THE WOMAN KEPT THE GUN NELL THE GUN FROM MY CHIN. "WE'RE NOT GOING TO ARGUE WITH YOU, NANETTE."

There was a man in the front seat of the van. Middle-aged. Black raincoat. Pitiless blue eyes, which he turned on me.

"What I care about is you shooting off your mouth about Rhode Island Red. You are not going to shoot off your mouth anymore."

For a second there—just a second—I forgot I was being held captive. I leaned forward eagerly. "You know what it is? I was only trying to find out what it means."

At his nod, the woman pushed the gun into my neck. My head slammed hard against metal. *You've been all kinds of set up,* I thought.

"I'm through talking," the grand inquisitor pronounced. "I hope you're through talking too. If you mention Rhode Island Red again, your big mouth won't be the only hole you've got in your head . . ."

HIGH NOTES AND HIGH PRAISE FOR
RHODE ISLAND RED

"Wholly delightful . . . the year's freshest crime debut."
—*GQ Magazine*

"A hot mystery debut whose jazzy prose riffs read poetic."
—**George P. Pelecanos**

"Gritty."
—*Kirkus Reviews*

"Breezy, sexy mystery . . . Nanette [is] charming and confident. . . . The details about music and musicians are well placed, and her down-and-out colleagues are an intriguing, believable bunch."
—*Publishers Weekly*

more . . .

"Jazzy."

"Extraordinary . . . smart . . . a good character-driven story with surprises. . . . Carter has added a refreshingly new kind of private dick to the market. . . . Nan, the engaging protagonist . . . is [an] always appealing character. Carter splices the straightforward detective genre with jazzy rhythms and an edgy, intimate narrative."

"Ripping good page-turner . . . gritty, cleverly done."

"A good one . . . kept me guessing to the very end, and the twist was authentic."

"A treat."

"Rapid-fire, staccato mystery . . . twists and turns like Charlie Parker playing."

"Spread the word . . . Carter has what impresses me more than just about anything in a crime writer: the practiced discipline needed to craft functional, human sentences that flow one into the next without embellishment or posturing. This is a writer at ease with herself and with the necessity . . . [of] telling a story. Well done."

Also by Charlotte Carter
Coq au Vin

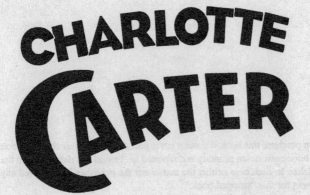

CHARLOTTE CARTER

Rhode Island Red

WARNER BOOKS

A Time Warner Company

WARNER BOOKS EDITION

This Warner Books Edition is published by arrangements with Serpent's Tail, 4 Blackstock Mews, London N4 and 180 Varick Street, 10th Floor, New York, NY 10014.

Cover design by Rachel McClain
Cover illustration by Paul Rogers

Warner Books, Inc.
1271 Avenue of the Americas
New York, NY 10020

Visit our Web site at
http://warnerbooks.com

A Time Warner Company

Printed in the United States of America

First Warner Books Printing: February, 1999

10 9 8 7 6 5 4 3 2 1

For the music my parents heard, and the music they did not.
And for Frank King.

Rhode Island Red

CHAPTER ONE
I Mean You

 Ask any Negro. They'll tell you: a woman does not play a saxophone.

Except for me.

Actually, I don't play sax. It's more like I noodle. I never studied the horn, but I can get through a "Stars Fell on Alabama" or a "Night and Day" with little or no problem. I was a far from brilliant student of the piano but I can sight read my way through a whole lot of Bach or Bud Powell. See, I'm naturally musical—not talented—I didn't say I was talented—just musical. At one point—what was I? Three? Four years old?—my father thought I might have been a genuine inheritor in that endless line of black musical geniuses.

But not too many of us blow tenor in front of the Off Track Betting Parlor on Lexington Avenue with a battered old hat inverted on the sidewalk. No, I think I pretty much have the exclusive on that one.

But, wait. Let me explain a few things.

I'm not a homeless beggar. I play music on the sidewalks of New York but I don't sleep there. I'm 5 feet 10 inches tall, I turned twenty-eight in January, I'm more or less a Grace Jones lookalike in terms of coloring and body type (she has the better waist, I win for tits), I'm the former second runner-up in the state spelling bee (I was twelve then), hold a degree in French with a minor in Music from Wellesley (scholarship all the way), and I live in a fairly low rent, nondescript walk-up at the edge of Gramercy Park, where that neighborhood starts to bleed into the Methodone-rich valley of drug treatment facilities, hospitals, and drooling academies, at First Avenue.

You know what jazz musicians are like. Always trying to stay cool in the face of the worst kind of hardships. Well, just a couple of days ago, I had come up against a pretty hard one. I was dumped—hard.

I thought I looked especially cool that day.

Mostly because of the two-hundred-dollar Italian shades Walter had mistakenly left in the apartment when he moved out—again. This break-up was not the kind of nuclear dogfight we had had in the past. It was just about that low-level hostility toward each other for months on end; that cold kind of resentment; that sex that's still good but just not right. And then one morning when he goes to work he's carrying a suitcase with his stuff in it along with his briefcase.

Not to worry: Walter Michael Moore had someplace else to go. He is very good at hedging his bets, always has been. He never let go of the small rent-controlled place up on Amsterdam and I was pretty sure that around the next corner there was another lady quite willing to sacrifice a little closet space for his buppy perfect Paul Stuart and Hugo Boss suits.

No, no need to worry about Walter. Matter of fact, *fuck*

Walter. It was yours truly who now had to worry about keeping body and soul together. Who needed Walt's four fifths of the rent and groceries like Abbott needed Costello. Who wasn't currently *employed*—okay? Who never really got the hang of saving money and had never once been accused of being too future-oriented.

I had long ago incinerated my bridges at the temp agency. The translation gigs I had depended on for the past year were drying up. And how could I ask my mother for anything when, one, she was struggling with bills herself and, two, I was lying through my teeth to her on a regular basis about the terrific part-time position I had teaching French at NYU?

Speaking of "Body and Soul," I was longing to hear it. Oh, I knew I wasn't ready to play it, I just wanted to hear it. If I kept practicing, I figured, I would be able to do a passable imitation of Ben Webster's licks on it. But it would be just that—an imitation, a homage.

Not that Webster, fabulous as he was, is god number one in my pantheon. There's Parker and Rollins and Coltrane . . . well, the list goes on endlessly. I think it's a good thing to have an open-ended pantheon. When it comes to the piano, though, it's Monk whom I have accepted as my personal savior. All that quirky, absent-minded professor, mad as a hatter, turn-everything-on-its-head brand of genius. Oh, do I love that man. And what about doomed, beautiful, young Clifford Brown with his enchanted horn and Miles with his evil self and—

I'm getting a request from the portly old alcoholic who swings by my corner a couple of times a day. "Violets for Your Fur," he wants to hear. How sweet. I play it and he gives me five bucks and blows me a kiss in the bargain. Bless his heart, as my mom would say.

Long day. Long day, today. Lot of time to think about all kinds of things: my last trip to France, a couple of years ago; that old white Saab that this guy Jean Yves had—sitting in it, waiting for him, eating french fries while he borrowed money from a wealthy friend who lived on the rue Madame; my old piano teacher, dead; the word I blew at the spelling bee—logarhithms; cigarettes, and how I missed them; Walter's chest, the same color as powdered cocoa and his chipped tooth and his mouth on me and soaping his back and the two of us going out to eat.

I know how much it irritated him when I shaved my head. It's odd, isn't it? Black men like white women's hair, and white guys like black women without hair. Not an iron law, I realize, but it's one of my theories that bears out time and again. Anyway, my locks are coming back nicely now. That kind of gamine look you saw in the magazines a couple of years ago. Only the rest of the body is more Masai warrior than Kate Moss.

Good thing I had those dark glasses. All those melancholy, lost, private things going through my head. Things I wouldn't want anybody to read in my eyes.

I went on playing but I was kind of on automatic pilot.

No doubt about it, I'd come way down in the world from my bourgeois roots.

So there I was on that September afternoon, trying to breathe some life into my limited repertoire of standards. "Mood Indigo" was getting no respect. Not even my spare, self-mocking medley of Monk favorites could impress the ignorant passers-by. In a desperate move, stealing Jimi Hendrix blind, I switched to "America the Beautiful."

Forget it. The streets were teeming with humorless patriots.

By four o'clock, I had about twenty-one bucks in the hat.

I really started to curse Walt about four-thirty.

People take quitting time seriously in this town. By six o'clock the street was empty. I knew I was licked; there wasn't going to be no Mount Everest of bills in my hat today. In the growing dark I bent down to collect the day's pathetic take.

"You can't play worth shit, man."

I looked up quickly to see who had spoken. He was a scrawny young white man, lounging against a parking meter and chuckling aloud. I noted his longish sandy hair, his brown suede jacket with fringe, and his dirty Converse running shoes. He looked to be about twenty-three or -four. He looked to stand about five-seven or -eight.

I stiffened. "What did you say, fool?"

He went on laughing at me, unfazed. "I said you sound like shit. And where did you get that horn at—L.L. Bean?" He began calmly adjusting the many cheap leather bands around each of his wrists.

It wasn't until that moment that I spotted his overage saxophone case. Damn—he *would* be a musician. So my humiliation was going to be complete. I didn't answer him but began to transfer the change to my pocket.

"You know, you'll never make any bread around here," he said, "even if you could play a lick. Too far east," he explained smugly. "You gotta go over to Fifth. Sixth and Seventh is good, too—up by Carnegie Hall."

Still ignoring him, I started downtown, toward my apartment.

"Wait a minute!" he called out suddenly. "Hey, where you going! Wait a minute."

I looked back over my shoulder. His voice and manner had suddenly changed from pesky terrier to lovesick Great Dane.

"Just a minute, willya. I gotta tell you something."

"What?"

He paused to take a cigarette out of the pack of Marlboro Lights he carried in the waistband of his black jeans. "I play . . . on the street . . . just like you. Well, not just like you. I'm good. But I just gotta tell you I . . . I'm desperately in love with you. Know what I mean? Totally. Desperate. I mean it, man. And if you don't take me home with you I'm going to just step in front of the downtown fuckin' bus."

"You got a token?" I asked and kept moving.

I'd gone only about ten paces when I heard a woman scream. I whirled.

He had leapt out about six feet into downtown traffic, in the path of the Lexington Avenue bus. It had swerved and just flicked his arm, but with enough force to slam him back onto the sidewalk about two feet from where I stood. He lay there on his back clutching his horn.

Shaken, I knelt and raised his head a few inches off the ground.

"Hey," he said, grinning, "I been watching you all day. My name is Sig. And you have nothing to worry about."

"*I* have nothing to worry about?"

"Yeah. My old lady put me out because I took a pledge of celibacy. So my love for you is pure. I want you for your mind." And he gave me an angelic, lying smile.

"What's the rest of this story?" I asked wearily.

"I need a place to crash, one night only. I'm tired as hell. I could use something to eat. You look kind. I was hoping you'd feel sorry for a fellow musician."

For a long moment I stared into his diamond bright green eyes. Then I let his head fall back onto the pavement. I asked myself, Nan, what is the stupidest conceivable decision you could make in this situation?

My next move seemed clear.

My apartment is a floor-through on First Avenue between Seventeenth and Eighteenth. Pretty good morning light. Not too noisy on the front. Furnished in high sharecropper chic.

Sig was cross-legged on the kitchen floor. It turned out his head was bleeding from the fall he'd taken, so he sat pressing a folded patch of gauze against his hair. He studied the walls while I put the finishing touches on one of my signature dishes—fresh sardines deep fried in Greek olive oil and thin linguine with garlic and little green peas.

"I like that one!" he said, pointing at the Huey Newton poster that I'd hung upside down.

"That one's great, too." He meant Lady Day near death, which had cost me about a hundred dollars to frame.

"I don't know about that one," he said doubtfully, nodding at Walter's autographed photo of Magic Johnson with his bad boy guru smile.

"Dinner," I announced. "Get up off the floor."

I set a steaming plate in front of him along with a cold glass of cheap white wine. He made a face.

"What is this? This is not the kind of stuff you feed a street musician. We need more protein . . . like cheeseburgers."

I cursed him in gutter French.

"Did you call me something bad?" He adjusted the makeshift headband he'd tied on in order to keep the gauze in position. "Well, that's okay. I still love you desperately."

I couldn't help but laugh. Up close, I could see that little Sig was quite a bit older than he looked at first glance—what said it were those little drinking lines around the base of his nose. There was something else that did not escape my notice: tell-tale wrinkles, dirty hair and all, little Sig was quite pretty. I wondered what he'd done to make his lady put him out.

He ate his food like a good boy, even paying me a compliment or two on it, after he got used to the taste.

"Sweetness," he said, wiping his mouth, "if you make a living playing that sax, I'm Louis Armstrong. Who are you really?"

"Really? My real name is Simone."

"No kidding? Simone what?"

"Signoret."

"Huh. That's kind of a pretty name."

This child, I decided, was from an outer sphere.

Then, while I did the dishes, he began to rattle on about the saxophone and all its glory. God, what a torrent of reverently uttered names and birthplaces, record dates and sidemen. Coleman and Prez and Bird and Sonny and Jug and Trane and Bippity Boppedy Boo. I finally sent him off for a shower, hoping it would calm him down.

I picked up the bunch of brown straps he'd taken off his wrists and left on the kitchen table. They were made of flimsy Indian leather, still stiff with newness, and the head of a bald eagle was embossed on each strap. It made me smile; I used to have a thing for cheap bracelets, too. And

I also liked wearing them in bunches. See, just wearing two or three of them won't get it. You have to put on dozens. For some reason, the sheer number of them cancels out their essential tackiness.

I lit one of Sig's cigarettes and sat down to look at my mail, all those bills I had no way of paying now that Walt and his salary were gone.

I had a second smoke and polished off the lousy chardonnay.

He reappeared twenty minutes or so later—calm, clean, hair slicked back and glistening, torso bared—and a nice torso it was—thin but basically flawless.

One of my extravagant white Fieldcrest bath towels was knotted low on his hips, and inside it, where stomach meets thigh, was a little palm tree. He looked at me while I looked at him.

"Ah," I said, and kept looking.

He smiled slyly. "I am your slave," he pronounced.

"Ah," I said.

"Where's the bedroom?"

"Mine?" I asked after a minute. "Or yours?"

"Ah," he said sadly, and shrugged.

Yes, thank God he was older and more sensible than he looked.

We took the old futon out of the hall closet and rolled it out on the living room floor.

"Listen, Sig," I told him as I turned out the light, "coffee's at seven-thirty. Then out you go."

"But I'm your slave—"

"Hey, Siggy? Being a person of color, that is not my favorite word in the English language."

I took his laugh as a sign that he was finally giving up.

"Gets pretty cool in here at night," I said. "Summer's over, you know."

"Guess I better put on my pants then."

"Guess you better."

Around 3 A.M. I woke up achy and shivering. I felt the cold air creeping around the corners of my room like a wild cat prowling a canyon. I wondered if that fool had gone during the night and left the apartment door open.

Furious, I walked into the kitchen. Sure enough, the door was wide open. I banged it shut . . . then banged it a second time, because the lock wouldn't catch.

I flipped on the light, all sorts of wild things in my mind—he'd robbed the shit out of me; he'd gone out for pizza and decided not to return, so someone else had robbed the shit out of me . . .

But no.

He was right there. On the floor.

With a blade sticking out of his throat.

I did the corny silent scream as my legs gave way and I began to sink. It took forever for my knees to finally hit the linoleum.

On the floor between us lay a small Velcro ankle holster with a blunt steel gray gun nestled inside it.

On the outside of the holster was a photo ID shrink wrapped in plastic. I pulled it closer with my foot and looked at the picture of Sig, who was in real life—or had been—Charles A. Conlin, of the New York Police Department.

CHAPTER TWO

In Walked Bud

Two uniformed cops came first. They looked at the body but didn't touch it.

The EMS guys came next. They touched but didn't move. Then along came one Detective Butko, who, to use the vernacular, took my statement. As we talked, the technicians started to file in—all looking as if they had TB. My little apartment, so private and anonymous until a few short hours ago, was swollen with city payrollers. All of them men. Loud and gross and way past the point of caring. The one slobbering all over my busted door looked ready to shed his old skin any minute.

"How come you didn't hear anything?" Butko asked me.

"For the same reason," I told him, "I wouldn't hear it if you played a rap song in this room right now."

My hatred for rap music was so overwhelming that I had actually developed the ability to tune it out—deny that it existed. I hated violent death just as much. Yet Sig's body was still there in my kitchen.

Then, about five-thirty in the morning, the clock stopped,

so to speak. The apartment was at capacity now, but it had grown strangely quiet. They were all standing around . . . waiting. Poor Sig/Conlin was waiting too, in his way.

I wanted nothing more at the moment than a piece of paper and pencil.

I mean, I know how crass it sounds, a young guy laying there dead and all. But since there was nothing anybody could do to change that, I thought the least I could do was get off a few lines about the thing. All the time I was speaking to Butko, the words were sort of floating across my eyes like they were being spat out of a teletype machine. Something like "Butterflies never die but just tremble and vanish." Lord! . . . butterflies trembling and vanishing would have made my grad school advisor at NYU vomit. But that was last year and this was this year.

I took down the big glass percolator my mother had given me. She had somehow managed to ignore every reminder over the years that I despised perked coffee and never used anything but a drip pot. I wonder where I get my willful nature from. For a few minutes everyone watched hypnotized while the glass pot bubbled and shook. I don't know when it happened, but a minute later I realized that all eyes had turned to me.

The nightgown I had on was right out of George Sand. Good cotton, good lace and loads of it, hand rolled hem, and diaphanous as hell. I looked down furtively and saw how clearly, aggressively, my dark breasts were outlined against the fabric. I felt a stab of shame for every time I had lain there, proud, loving it, while a man delighted in them.

Each and every one of these strange men was looking at my nipples—focusing—concentrating—on them. And it meant nothing to them that they were dealing with a lady who was going to do the definitive translation of *A Season in Hell*.

I wondered briefly, insanely, if this was going to escalate one glance, one wordless movement at a time, until I ended up raped and torn apart and dead—framed, conveniently, for Officer Conlin's murder. It would be one of those grotesque cover-ups no one would find out about for forty years.

> *For whom should I whore?*

The first line of my Rimbaud translation came back to me then.

> *For whom should I whore*
> *Which beast shall I worship?*
> *What Madonna should I ravish?*
> *What heart should I profane?*
> *What lies should I live by?*
> *In whose blood should I swim?*

The committee had thrown the thesis right back in my face thanks to that translation.

I was relieved to see that the men had stopped staring. Except Sig, of course. How long were they going to leave that dead man there?

"For godsakes," I said to Butko, "can't you at least pull that knife out of his neck?"

"Not a knife, honey," he said, searching for sugar in the cabinet above my refrigerator. "It's an ice pick."

Who was he calling honey, and where the fuck did he think he was—Little Rock?

Before I could ask, a black man burst through the half-open door, scattering lab men like milk bottles. He had a baseball hat turned around backwards on his head. And he was wearing painter's pants and a dirty flannel shirt buttoned right up to the neck. His Fu Manchu moustache and battered old guitar completed the picture.

"Okay, Leman, Okay!" shouted Butko, gripping the man by the arm. Leman shook him off violently. He walked over to the covered body and straddled it.

I heard him ask the corpse in a weird voice: "Charlie, is that you?"

The rest of what he said was lost to me. Just muffled, strangling sounds—"Oh, my, oh, my," I thought I heard him say. Or perhaps it was "Oh, man, oh, man."

In a minute he began to cry. It was something wild and hideous.

And then he picked up the guitar and smashed it into smithereens against the cabinet. Every soul in the room ran—ran like hell—away from this Leman.

I sat in the living room on the tatty divan I had paid my neighbor's kids to haul upstairs last year. The cops and the rest of the men had slowly filtered back into the kitchen and were wrapping things up. I heard the labored, inevitable sound of Sig being dragged across the kitchen in his plastic shroud. Finally, he was out of my house. The sun was out now.

"Tell me a story."

I looked up into the dark wide face of Detective Leman Sweet. He hulked over me, sucking the air out of the room.

"I already told him," I replied, pointing to Butko.

"Tell me!"

I did. The whole story. All the while staring into the bottom of my coffee cup.

Leman Sweet grinned when I finished talking. He moved even closer to me and undid the top button of his shirt. "You're a lying cunt," he stated.

I got to my feet. He hit me with the heel of his hand, crashing against my shoulder and knocking me back down. The cold coffee in my mug splashed out onto his face. I looked to Butko for help. He never moved.

"Did he fuck you?" Sweet asked.

"No."

"Yeah, he did. Charlie fucked you. Did you like that?"

I said nothing. My knees were trembling.

"You like little white boys, don't you?"

I said nothing.

"Answer me! You . . . like . . . white . . . dick . . . don't you!"

I figured there was nothing to lose. He was going to kill me, anyway. So I got one in: "Actually, I prefer Samoans."

Butko laughed.

"You got Charlie all hot, didn't you?" Sweet went on. "You turned a trick, didn't you? What are you—a college girl? You movin' on up, don't like to do it the old-fashioned way. You want it all—fast. You don't want to push a mop no more, huh? Got to have it fast. Expensive. So you can keep that cue ball head of yours all clean and smelling sweet."

Maybe he will exhaust himself in a few minutes, I thought. If I just sit here. Maybe he'll stop and go away. Maybe he'll just die.

He caught sight of my sax just then. He walked over to it in its open case.

"This yours? You play it?"

"Yes it's mine, yes I play it."

He kicked the case halfway across the room.

"You play it on the street?"

"Anything in particular you'd like to hear?"

He came rushing at me.

"Leman!" Butko shouted.

He got a hold of himself. "Take a good look at me, girl. Because you going to see me again. And you going to talk to me again . . . Understand?"

No! I wanted to scream it into his face. No, I do not understand, you moron! But I just sat there.

At last, he backed off. I heard him cussing as he ran down the stairs.

Detective Butko looked at me for a long time without speaking. "You better change the lock," he said finally. "Just to be on the safe side." I guess that was about as close as I was going to come to getting some concern or sympathy from our public guardians. I chuckled audibly and Butko gave me a funny look.

He walked back into the kitchen. A few minutes later he was gone.

I went and closed the door quietly behind him—for all the good that was going to do. I laughed when I thought back to that question Sig had asked me: Who are you really? I should have been the one to ask him that.

What I wanted to do was rage and scream and put my fist through a wall. But there had been enough violent acting-out in my home. I was wrung out—and just really sad.

I looked up searchingly into Billie's cloudy eyes. She knew!

CHAPTER THREE

Nutty

The sleep I was getting was more trouble than it was worth. I went and fixed a tray and had my coffee in bed. And eventually I got up and put some Monk on the turntable. Thelonious at his quirkiest—all the old ballads turned on their head. Boy, did that fit in with my life.

It could be worse, I kept telling myself while I located the vacuum cleaner and filled the scrub bucket. It could be worse. Though I couldn't think how. Well, yeah, I could have been the corpse. That would be worse. Or Leman Sweet, instead of calling me the "c" word, could have said I looked like Odetta, as some drunk asshole had done in a restaurant once. Nothing against that venerable lady, but I do not appreciate being taken for a sixty-year-old folk singer.

On my hands and knees, I scrubbed away at the blood-stain. Then I gathered up the splinters from Sweet's guitar. I wondered what street corner he played on—that street I was never going to walk down as long as I lived.

I also wondered what two detectives were doing posing as funky street musicians.

The building super knocked on the door and wanted to know what had happened here last night . . . why all the cops and what kind of trouble had I plunged the building into.

"A corpse," I told him.

"What corpse?"

"A dead man's corpse."

"But who was the dead corpse?"

"Sig," I said.

"This is very bad. This is terrible."

I agreed.

He shook his head, promising me retribution from the landlord.

I finished the washing-up. The place looked a little frazzled around the edges, but it was clean. Now I was hungry. But the cupboard was bare. I didn't have the strength to face the supermarket. Even the easy way out—the corner deli—would mean cooking eggs and toasting bread. Too much.

I decided to take a nap. If I felt just as lazy when I woke up, I'd go ahead and blow five bucks in the coffee shop.

As I slogged over to the divan, I saw my poor sax and its case lying abandoned in the corner. I went over and straightened the instrument in its carrier. Then I pulled it back to the spot it had originally occupied on the floor, before Officer Sweet's temper had sent it flying.

Something was sticking out of the bowl of my sax. I peered in there. For godsakes—it was a dirty sock! At least that's what it looked like—a long, dirty white sock.

I pulled on the tip of the sock. At first it wouldn't budge. But then, slowly, it began to loosen and move. Then it became stuck again. There was something hard and ridged in the toe, something like a sewing spool. I gave it one good yank, and the whole sock popped out. And then another one rolled out after it.

The first one felt heavy in my hand. The way I imagined a sap would heft in one's hand. I had never seen a sap in my life, but it's something they're always talking about in those old black and white detective movies.

I shook out the sock. What I had arrayed before me on the rug were six tightly rolled wads of fifty-dollar bills fastened with rubber bands. About 100 fifties to each roll. That came to five thousand dollars a wad.

Sock number two was identical. All together there were twelve rolls.

There was sixty thousand dollars—in cash—in fifties—inside my little sax.

I backed away from the heap and collapsed onto the divan. This was too much. Too crazy—even for me.

Only one person could have filled my stocking like that: Siggy. Also known as Officer Charlie Conlin.

While I was asleep, he was playing Santa Claus. And they killed him—those evil elves, or whoever. I wondered if he knew all along they were coming for him.

Why me? Why my poor little beaten-up sax?

Any way you answered those unanswerables, it meant trouble.

I knew what I had to do. Gather up all that money and run as fast as I could to the local precinct, hand it over to the police . . . to Detective Leman Sweet. Whom I wanted to see again like I wanted to be buried up to my neck and left to die in the desert.

Besides, he wouldn't believe a word I said. He'd say I murdered Sig for the money. Never mind that it didn't make sense for me to kill him and then turn around and surrender the loot. Leman Sweet would probably make it his life's work to see me hang for the killing. It was as though he and I were living proof of that popular babble about the enmity between black men and women. Circumstance . . . history . . . had made us instant, mortal enemies. There was nothing we could do about it. And it was very pathetic.

But maybe I was letting my imagination run rampant. Even somebody as out of control as Sweet had to do some logical thinking. After all, he was a detective. But, who knew? Who knew what someone like that would think or do? To be black and a cop, you've got to be pretty weird.

I needed help. Advice. A cool head. I had to speak to Aubrey.

Aubrey is my oldest friend. We grew up together, the children in the only two black families on a Spanish-speaking block in East Elmhurst, Queens.

I was smart. In fact, I was so smart that the papers wrote about me. I was one of those obnoxious child prodigies whose exploits are fillers for the *Daily News*. At seven I could add figures in the time it takes to light a match. I picked up languages in half a day. And I could play "Misty" in synch with Erroll Garner. The trouble was, all I wanted to do was dance. And I couldn't. And can't. To this day.

Aubrey was . . . well, not smart. Dumb was the blunt, casually cruel word the kids used. Strange how she turned out to be so pulled together. While I tend to be in tatters a good once a day. Where did that child prodigy shit get me?

Anyway, the one thing Aubrey could do was dance. Man, could she dance. And she was going to teach me how to move. She was supposed to help me become this ravishing, knockout irresistible, Folies Bergère fandancing, headdress wearing, Jo Baker clone. Forget it. I cannot move. And the closest I ever got to ravishing the French was the day I stood on a chair in a café on the rue de Savoie and recited Rimbaud from memory. I was very drunk and showing my stuff in the company of this coke head academic from Toulouse.

Aubrey is still dancing. She is one of the bigger draws at Caesar's Go Go Emporium, which is exactly the kind of place it sounds like, located on a dirty street down where Chinatown meets hyper-hip Tribeca.

She performs topless—and damn near bottomless—and usually clears more than a thousand dollars a week, about two hundred of which gets reported. Aubrey is one of the strongest women I know. She is also a beauty. I love her very much. And she ain't dumb.

She works all night and sleeps all afternoon. I felt bad about calling her, waking her, but I did and said I'd be over in forty minutes.

I stuffed the rolls of fifties back into the socks and the socks back into the sax and closed the case on the whole works.

I entered the glass-walled, opulent lobby of Aubrey's Upper Broadway building. I had been told that Reverend Ike, a you-can-get-yourself-a-million-dollars-if-you-send-me-twenty-bucks kind of sharpie, lived here with a large entourage. Occasionally one of the fatuous doormen, of which there were many, mistook me for one of the reverend's harem. It escaped me why Aubrey, who didn't hook, chose to live in a place where half the neighbors were turning tricks of one kind or another.

Up I went in the supersonic space capsule. Aubrey was waiting in the doorway. How did a woman who kept such ungodly hours manage to look so unpuffy? Her permed hair was tousled as if someone had arranged it that way for the camera. She turned that slow burning smile of hers up a notch when she saw me step off the elevator. She was wearing a long white silk thing and a pair of frou frou white mules—looking very much the star.

On those few occasions when I'm in the Emporium watching her dance, I see how much of a star she is. There's something so hard-edged about the other dancers. They've got dumb routines—fake s & m crap or 1960s hippie fantasies with tie-dyed G-strings—or they just look like tired junkies.

But Aubrey is different. Commanding yet soft. Soft shoulders, soft, insinuating movements. I've heard the way the men take in their breath at the first sight of her toffee colored thighs. She is so quiet when she's up there. It seems to make them hush as well.

We told my mother that Aubrey is a cashier at a posh downtown restaurant. I have no idea whether Mom really bought that, but she behaves as if she has.

"God, Aubrey," I began apologizing. "I woke you up. Sorry, honey."

"You in trouble?"

"Big trouble," I said, closing the apartment door.

"*The* trouble?"

"No. Worse."

"What's worse than being pregnant?"

"This," I said, and I opened the sax case and pulled the rolls out of the socks and dumped them on her white leather sofa.

She picked up one of the wads, dazed. "This is trouble?"

"Yeah."

"Where'd it come from?"

"A dead guy."

"He gave it to you?"

"In a way."

"Before or after he was dead?"

"A little of both. He was a cop."

"Get outta town, Nan."

"No, I'm not kidding. He was under cover. He was working right near where I was playing yesterday. He said he was a musician."

"What do Walter say about it all?"

"Nothing. Walter moved out a few days ago."

"Good. That silly motherfucker needed to move somewhere." Aubrey walked into the kitchen then and came back with one of those plastic jugs of freshly squeezed orange juice and two glasses. She drank hers. I followed suit dutifully, hating it, and told her the story.

"So that's why I'm disturbing you, Aubrey. Help me figure out what to do."

"Nothing to figure, Nan. You got sixty thousand dollars."

"But what was a cop doing with sixty thousand in rolled-up fifties?"

"Musta been working nights." She laughed at her own joke. Then she said: "Maybe if you read the paper once in a while . . ." Her voice trailed off as she picked delicately through the cigarettes in the glass box on the coffee table.

"What paper? What are you talking about?"

"The newspaper, girl. I remember seeing something in the *Post* a few weeks ago about the bums and the street musicians getting beat up in the subways. Paper said they gone be using decoys to try to catch whoever's doing it. That's probably what your friend was. One of the decoys. Pretending like he played a fiddle on the street."

"A sax," I corrected, "not a fiddle. And he seemed to know his stuff."

"Whatever. Fuck what he played. If the other cops don't know about the cash, it's yours."

I don't know what Aubrey was reading on my face just then, but suddenly she stopped talking and regarded me with wariness.

"Nan, don't tell me," she finally said. "Don't tell me you gone give it to the police. Not after all the shit I been hearing about Paris in the fall and what you wouldn't give to get back there . . . Look, take that money and buy your ticket."

"But what about his wife and kids, Aubrey?"

"Do he have a wife and kids?"

"Well, he told me he had a woman—an old lady, he said. He must've meant his wife."

She shook her head in disgust.

"He said his lady had kicked him out," I continued. "I don't know if it was a woman he knew as part of his cover—or whether she was for real in his life. But if she was real, then why should it be me who . . . I mean, she should get it."

"Get what?"

"The money, of course."

"We should all get some money, girlfriend."

I walked over to one of her windows and stared out. What a wonderful view! Out across the park and all the way east.

"He said he was desperately in love with me." I waited for her laugh, but I didn't hear it. "You think that's possible, Aubrey? You think he really wanted me to have that money?"

"Go to Paris, Nan."

"Come with me. I'll show it to you."

She waved me off derisively. As if the very idea of Aubrey Davis on foreign soil were preposterous.

I didn't say anything more about the money. Instead I went to the shelf and started rooting around in search of an Etta James cassette I felt like hearing. While I looked for it, I sang under my breath, mocking Aubrey, but in a friendly way: "When my soul was in the lost and found, you came along to claim it."

We had a grim joke when we were young. Rather than come out and admit she had been off with a man, Aubrey used to say she'd been down at the bus depot all night, waiting at the lost and found for her mother, who was sure to come back one day and inquire about her.

So, as far as Aubrey was concerned, it was simple—I should take the money and run. Not even run—saunter—to Paris. But then, Aubrey was pretty fearless. As for me, I may crave adventure, but things can scare me. And not just Leman Sweet. I was scared that one way or another those big fat rolls of fifty-dollar bills were going to end up choking me. Even I am continually surprised at how close to the surface my sense of Christian guilt and terror remains.

No, I wasn't going to buy a ticket to Paris. Not yet. And no, I wasn't going to the police. Not yet. What I had to get started on first was finding little Mrs. Sig and all her poor children.

CHAPTER FOUR

Rhythm-a-ning

 I might have gone a little overboard on the outfit that morning. What I was going for was street waif. But I ended up looking more like a parody of a young civil rights worker in the 1960s—and a male specimen at that. I was wearing my faded James Farmers with one strap safety pinned; my prototype Stokely Carmichael shades; a black cotton turtleneck; and lace-up shitkickers.

Sig, in his wisdom, had warned me that I'd never make any money in this spot. And sure enough, the breakfast in a bag crowd was once again passing me by. Partly my fault, though: they must have thought I was nuts to be blowing Coltrane blues licks that early in the morning. Who the hell wants to be moved into that kind of space before they even *get* to the job?

But this time I wasn't out there for the money. I was there for Sig and Mrs. Sig—and for my conscience, which I call Ernestine. Because my do-your-liberated-shit-but-later-pray-you-ain't-gonna-burn-in-hell hypocrisy rates a dorky name like that. Kind of tough to be a wanton when four hundred years of history have been grooming you for that place on the church pew.

A kick from old Ernestine made me suddenly think of my mother. I think maybe she's a little put out that I haven't been calling her so often lately. But she doesn't get too mad, because at least her terminally quirky child is busy with honorable work. Teaching French lit at NYU. Or so Mom thinks, sitting out there in Queens. Damn, I've told a lot of lies to that woman in my lifetime . . . little lies, big lies . . . sometimes for next to no reason. And I've no fucking idea why I do it.

How did I come to be this compulsive liar? It must have started with that imagination of mine—the one Mom thought was so wonderful when I was little. The one that got me out of Elmhurst and took me to Paris. That always seems to land me in some new pot of soup no matter how sensibly I'm trying to comport myself.

Anyway, if the morning crowd thought I was nuts, they weren't far wrong. I was running the streets of Manhattan with sixty grand zippered into my overalls.

I circled like a Comanche that day. From Nineteenth Street on the south to Sixty-first Street on the north. From Park on the east side to Ninth Avenue on the west. Then back in the other direction. I was looking for street players. Looking for leads to Sig's lady friend.

And I found street players, in all their infinite variety. Jazz is hardly the only idiom of street music. I figured, however, that the kind of music they played was a lot less important than how they played it—outside, for tips. I thought there would be an automatic brotherhood among the various genres. So I talked to them all. Sax players. Violinists. Steel drummers. Flutists. Guitarists. Truth is, I had heard some pretty good stuff by the time I decided to knock off for a while. But I hadn't found a single musician who knew Sig or the Mrs.

After lunch, which was a sodden piece of microwaved spinach quiche I had at a coffee bar in midtown, I headed for Grand Central Station.

I made my way leisurely through the cavernous rotunda. It had been longer than I realized since I'd been in there. God, how the place had changed! The homeless and the all-purpose psychos, who had for a time transformed the terminal into a haven for lost souls, like something out of nineteenth-century London, had disappeared. The station had been face-lifted within an inch of its life: murals restored, ceilings repainted, brass burnished and shining like new shoes. This was the Deco era Grand Central of a high-budget movie.

And then, as if to underscore the illusion, the music began.

A saxophone—and a very accomplished one indeed—was treating the crowds to "Out of Nowhere." I followed the melody, the music growing louder as I neared its source. As soon as this guy finished playing, whoever he might turn out to be, I would start my rote interrogation—Hey, man, you play pretty. Know a white musician who calls himself Sig?

But that's where the screenplay took an unexpected turn. When I was a few feet away from the soloist, I saw that he wasn't alone. Nor was he your average street player. He was part of a combo of middle-aged men in uber conservative Brooks Brothers suits. On a folding table nearby they had set, not a hat for donations, but a briefcase, lid open, containing a couple of dozen copies of their latest CD. I looked at the sign next to the case, which listed each of their names and announced that this free lunchtime concert was being sponsored by the City Arts Council as a courtesy to the patrons at Grand Central Station—your basic quality of life innovation. The trio was well known to the so-called jazz cognoscenti. They played all the smart clubs uptown and were unerringly tasteful. No way would any of them know a scruffy guy like Sig.

I kept walking, past the tasteful strains of the next number, but threw a dented quarter into the briefcase, just to put a little shit in the game. I headed down one of the long corridors toward the revolving door that let out onto Vanderbilt Avenue.

Two young black men sporting matted Rasta braids had set up a card table against the window of an empty store in the corridor. One was loudly touting the myriad wares spread out on the table top, at the same time keeping a wary eye out for the cops who might come along at any moment and roust them.

I made a hurried survey of the merchandise—the usual crap: scarves, incense, factory second gym socks, ear muffs, headbands, Afro picks, and so on.

"A mufflah for ya, Sweetart?" the cuter one of them pitched me. "Genuine mohair, sistah, keep you warm when I'm not thah to do the job."

"How much?" I asked.

"Five."

"Genuine mohair, huh?"

"I look like a liar, mon?"

I chuckled, flirting a little. "No need to get into personalities."

He looked prepared to press his case, but I had stopped

listening by then. A particular group of items displayed on a plaster replica of a human arm had suddenly captured all my attention.

"What are those?" I asked, pointing.

"For you lovely wrist, lady. Two fa each. Three fa five."

I gave him five bucks and lifted off three of the wrist bands. Stiff Indian leather embossed with an eagle's head. The same ones Siggy was wearing.

"Let me help you," Mr. Smooth Salesman offered, expertly tying the bands on my wrists and all but copping a feel as he did so.

I took an even closer look at the bracelets. No doubt about it, these were the kind that Charlie Conlin had left on my kitchen table while he showered.

"Thanks a lot," I said innocently. "Now I want something else."

He grinned and passed his hand over the table in a gesture of magnanimousness. "Just you tell me, sistah. What else you want today?"

"I want you to tell me if you had a skinny white guy buy a lot of these lately. He would have been carrying a saxophone case most likely. Long hair. Young."

He cast a glance over at the other man and then turned his eyes back to me.

"Come on, sistah," he said derisively, "why you want a white mon when you have me?"

"You're very good," I said, and I meant it, actually. "But I've got to catch a train. Do you know the man or not?"

"Know nobody," the second guy spoke up then, a frost in his voice like they don't often get down Jamaica way.

"Oh really?" I said pleasantly, a little frightened but brazening it out. "Well, I think maybe you do."

"No no," cutey protested, still good natured. "We don't know your mon, sistah."

"You know what else I think?" I replied.

"What?"

"You look like a liar, mon."

He smiled wickedly. I took a ten out of my wallet and placed it on the table.

The second guy just shook his head.

"Okay, fellas," I said with a sigh, "I've got to make a quick decision here. I've got three phrases running around in my head. And I don't know which one is going to get me my answer the fastest when I start screaming. So let me try all three of them out on you. Number one: rape! Number two: vendor's license. Number three: green card."

Salesman Two started for me at that moment, but the smoothie put up a staying hand. "Mon didn't buy them," he said to me, voice suddenly affectless. "We give them to him for being lookout when we work Penn Station. He hang with old dude name of Wild Bill. They hustle, same as us. Okay, sistah?"

"Just fine," I said.

"Sorry to see you go, Sweetart."

Later that afternoon, a commuter in a tan raincoat—of all people—led me out of the wilderness. Just before he turned into Penn Station, the man called out to a musician standing nearby, "How's it going, Wild Bill?" and pressed a couple of bucks into the guy's pocket.

Wild Bill was trumpeting something that might have been pretty and autumnal if it weren't for the bitter hootiness in his tone. He reminded me of a mezzo past her prime, straining hideously for the same note that had once poured out of her throat like good vodka over ice.

The man who was playing looked, in fact, more like a clowned-out decoy at the rodeo than a jazz musician.

He wasn't young. But through the zigzags of white in his hair I could plainly see the remnants of flaming Malcolm X red. *Poil de carotte*, as we say in French.

The map of the colored man in America was written on his face. Yes, the black past was there, but there was something else.

I approached him in the same way I'd done with all the other musicians I'd interviewed during the day—walking up close to the person, listening attentively to his number, and then, without making too big a deal of it, leaving a donation in the hat or instrument case at the feet of the player. Then I leaned in casually and asked if by any chance he knew a white guy named Sig who blew alto.

Wild Bill laid his trumpet in its case, on top of my five. He straightened his dirty scarlet tie and checked his beaten-up shoes for scuffs . . . *and* adjusted his suit jacket and pinched the pleat in one greasy trouser leg. All without making a second's worth of eye contact with me.

I was beginning to feel like a housefly.

When I repeated my question about Sig, he deigned to acknowledge me. Wild Bill looked me up and down. But there was no hint of lasciviousness in his glance.

"I was wondering if you've seen Sig lately," I said politely.

"Yeah, I saw him . . . . Have you seen a beautician lately?"

Aha. So that was what I'd glimpsed in his face: he was mean.

When he was through cackling, he turned his head slightly, coughed and lit a cigarette.

I let him have that one. He knew Sig. I couldn't afford to unsheathe my rapier wit just now. Instead, I pressed on in the same pleasant tone. "When was it that you saw him, Wild Bill?"

"Two, three days," he offered. Like we were friends now.

"Wow," I said. "I've got a gig for him but I can't find him anywhere. Friend of mine wants him to play at his wedding. Any idea where his lady is . . . uh . . . whatsher-name?"

"Inge."

"Right, Inge. Know where she is? I could just give the message to her."

" 'Message' is just about right, baby. You look like the mailman in those threads."

Okay, that made two. I've never been a baseball fan, but everybody knows, three strikes and you're dead.

Still, I remained calm and good humored. And in a few minutes—thank the baby Jesus—Wild Bill grew tired of me. And just told me straight out, in plain English, no more zaps, that I would find Siggy's girlfriend near the school on Twenty-sixth and Seventh.

The "school" was the Fashion Institute of Technology.

The street was popping with activity: traffic bombing then crawling down Seventh Avenue, students resplendent in their downtown anti-fashion chic, luncheonette busboys in dirty aprons, wealthy ladies hailing cabs to all manner of late afternoon assignations in Soho. And then there was Inge.

She was seated on an old camp stool, her appreciative little audience forming a semicircle about her. There was her hat. There was her sax. There were her dead blue eyes and her dirty blond hair. There was her big rust-colored seeing eye dog . . . Lord have mercy she was blind.

She was playing "September Song." She was awful. But a white man was crying anyway. I waited out her set, trying to decide what to say to her. She treated us to a touchingly incompetent "Lost in the Stars." Then she tackled "Speak Low." And finished up, after that mini Kurt Weill festival, with a few pitiful riffs of "Cherokee." Damn, thought I, life is strange.

The people dispersed and she began to feel her way through the take in her hat. In a minute she stopped, cocking her head in my direction. But she remained silent, the smallest little smile on her lips.

Finally I spoke up. "Inge?"

"Yes?"

Asked and answered. Now what was I going to say? I wasn't ready.

"You're Siggy's friend, aren't you?" I improvised.

At the mention of his name her hand went up to the top button of her denim jacket. "Yes. Who's there?"

I was trying to pull some kind of semi-coherent lie together, but my mind wasn't turning over fast enough.

"Who's there?" she asked again. "Who is it?"

"My name is Ann. I—I'm a friend of Sig's."

"Where is he? Where's he been?"

There were freckles across the bridge of her nose. She became prettier the longer you looked at her. In fact she looked a little like Sig.

"Listen, Inge, I need to talk to you."

The dog at her feet seemed to look up expectantly at me. He was massive and sad-looking, and when he got to his feet it was as if they hurt him.

"I need to talk to you alone. Can we go someplace private?" I asked.

She snorted, as if I'd said something funny. Maybe the whole world is private if you're blind.

"I live close," she said. Inge packed up quickly and then leaned down to give a gentle tug on the dog's kerchief. "Let's go home, Bruno. Good boy."

With every step, Bruno threatened to get himself tangled up in her legs—almost tripping her—but she walked on nimbly.

I followed her wordlessly through the streets, too embarrassed to offer my arm at the crosswalk. The sax was plainly not this girl's calling. I wondered if she could sing, wondered if she had some kind of crazed Ray Charles fantasy working—hey, I'm soulful, I'm hip, I'm blind. Or maybe it was Sig who had that particular fantasy. Perhaps that had been part of his attraction to her. I flashed pruriently on the two of them making love, her willowy body moving under him, breath clogging, eyes staring at nothing. Well, maybe not at nothing; how did I know what she saw?

She lived in a brownstone between Sixth and Broadway. On the ground floor was a wholesale florist. We walked up a flight and then straight back to a plain, big, square of a room at the end of a hallway. Little furniture except a bed and chair and a plush little mattress for Bruno.

Inge kicked out of her high boots and lit a Newport 100.

"You're going to tell me bad news," she announced. "You're here to tell me something has happened to Sig."

The dog watched me carefully, seeming to wait for my reply before he settled his weight down onto the floorboards.

I gave up on the elaborate story I'd been working on. And merely said, "He's dead, Inge."

She moaned once and then fell silent. She smoked furiously for a minute.

"I knew it," she said by and by. "I knew it. The minute I heard your voice on the street. What happened?"

"He was murdered. It was—I mean, it looks as if it was a robbery gone wrong."

I waited for her tears—or something. But no—she went on puffing, biting into her bottom lip every now and then.

In a minute, she held the pack out to me. I took one gratefully, continuing to watch her face.

"What will you do?" I said after a few minutes.

"Nothing. I don't know. I didn't know him that long."

"Did you love him?"

She laughed abruptly. Then I saw the tears in the corners of her eyes.

"Inge, I feel terrible about what happened. Sig was in my . . . neighborhood when it happened. I just know he'd want me to come and tell you about it. And to help—help you out in any way I could."

She sat down then. "What did you say your name was?" she said wearily. "Angela?"

"Ann."

"Um. So Sig told you about me?"

"That's right. The last time we met, he did."

"I don't remember Sig talking about you. You a musician too?"

"Yes."

"What?"

"I blow tenor. Not too good, though. Sig was helping me."

"Can I make you a cup of coffee?"

"Why don't you just rest. I'll get it," I said. "Just tell me where things are."

"Ann?"

"What?"

"You have a good voice."

"Thank you."

"You know what?" she said, sounding like a six-year-old.

"What?"

"I'm sleepy now."

Inge slept for a half hour or so. Bruno kept an eye on me as I drank my coffee and toured the poor room.

I didn't know much about blindness or blind people. I thought they all read best sellers in Braille. So I was surprised to find, in the rickety, badly painted little bookcase near the bathroom, a few paperbacks, a couple of public library books and several other texts and magazines—even a couple of flesh rags—all in normal print. I also spotted a couple of well worn steno pads with mindless doodles penciled on the front covers.

I picked up one of the library books. *Days of Luxe: Luxury Liners on the Hudson Piers* read the cover. *The Irish of Hell's Kitchen, 1909–1969* read another.

I looked at a couple of the other titles: *Life and Death on the New York Docks* and *A Complete History of the Stevedores Union.*

How weird. No accounting for what people like to read. I wondered if someone came over and read to Inge regularly. And then it occurred to me that the books had to have belonged to Sig.

Of course. Not that I'd have pegged him for any kind of scholar, either.

When Inge woke she looked utterly lost. I waited while she washed up and then we went out for a pizza, Bruno in tow.

I was drinking alone in a tavern in the middle of the day. Something no properly raised black woman would ever do—it was acting nasty, acting like trash. And not a particularly nice tavern at that.

But I needed a bourbon, bad, and I needed to think.

So I had found little Mrs. Sig. And her fatherless baby— that would be Bruno in the cartoon version of this story.

Now what was I going to do about it?

Inge and Bruno were going to have it tough without Siggy. But it looked like they'd had it just as tough with him. Sig looked like any other down on his luck musician when I met him, yet he had plenty of money. Money as dirty as a tenement toilet, I wagered. But he hadn't used it, and he hadn't shared it with Inge. She didn't seem to have a clue to who he really was, no inkling he was a cop. I wondered if there was a legitimate Mrs. Sig somewhere— a real wife.

What to do? I could mail Inge a couple of hundred bucks anonymously. I could say it was from an old fan. Or I could just forget about her—try to, anyway. I could follow Aubrey's line of reasoning, too: finders, keepers. After all, Conlin left the money in my house, not Inge's. Truth was, I didn't know whether he'd meant to give a dime to

Inge or the legitimate Mrs. He may even have been fixing to dump the both of them. Yeah—nice guy.

That was just it, though. I'm under no illusion that I'm the queen of mature judgment, but I don't pick bad guys, heartless bastards. They might be fuck ups, they might be dumb, they might have a little larceny in their hearts, drink too much, think a little too highly of themselves for their own good, but nine times out of ten they *are* nice. And I couldn't imagine one of them sponging off a hapless blind girlfriend and then stiffing her when he hit the jackpot. There had to be a reason Sig hadn't told Inge about that money yet.

Yes, I had compassion for blind Inge. But I had to learn how to have a little compassion for poor little Nanette, too. Who needed a break. Who was about to fall on some pretty tough times herself, now that Walter had split.

Sure, a couple of hundred bucks in a plain brown wrapper would be just fine for Inge. Hell, I wouldn't turn it down if I were in her place.

I heard Ernestine whispering then: *Honey, Some doors are closed for a good reason. Crack this one a little bit more, and your heart's truly gone be ready for Satan.*

I called for another bourbon, no ice, asked the bartender for change and purchased a pack of Winston Lights from the machine. Except for my ongoing bumming of smokes from anybody I happened to be sitting across from, I had been off cigarettes for two years. Goddamn. Why did they make cigarettes taste so goddamn good if you weren't supposed to smoke the goddamn things?

The bourbon was awfully tasty too—with just a little water, no ice, no, no ice—mellow. Like me. Like Mellow Nan. No more No No Nanette. *Oui, Oui.* South of fucking

France. Little farmhouse. Field of lilac. Hot summer sun. String bikini. Real vegetables. *Vin rouge* to die.

Aubrey would scoff at this dilemma of mine. Fuck compassion, she'd say. Aubrey was mighty wise about life. Maybe I had no business doubting her on this one. Maybe my only dilemma was whether to take Air France or Sabena. American Express Travelers Checks or Cook's. France by rail or rent a car?

Ernestine was going to have my ass for this.

Two drivers took a pass on me before I could catch a cab home. I must have looked drunker than I was. But on the other hand, in the daytime it's always 50-50 whether a taxi will stop for me. I don't look straight enough to be a bougie bank exec, but I don't exactly look like I'm gonna take them to the South Bronx either. Sometimes the black drivers are just as bad as the white. I stand there on the curb wishing I was Sissy Spacek in *Carrie*. Just picturing that fucking yellow car skidding on two wheels into a concrete wall and blowing sky high and me watching the conflagration with a serene little smile on my lips. Witnesses, officer? No, sorry, I didn't see a thing.

Of course, when I'm in my night finery, it's a different story. I've caused more than one pile-up in my leather bustier.

The kitchen table was covered with newspapers, all of them turned to the travel section. I'd bought them to compare airline prices.

I'd taken the money and put it all in my knapsack, which I then propped up in the chair across from me. The bag looked for all the world like a puffed-up midget sitting there waiting for coffee to be served. When the telephone rang, I looked over at it, as though asking, Now who can that be?

Walter.

He begged me not to hang up on him, as I'd done late last night. He said he *had* to talk to me. He missed me so much he couldn't function. He *had* to see me.

I'm getting ready for a trip, I told him.

Just to see me once before I went off. I said I don't know—that fatal phrase: they always know they've got you when you say I don't know. Women are dumb a lot of the time: it's not a pretty thing to face, but there it is. I said I don't know, but I did know: he was going to come over. And we were going to talk. And we were going to end up in bed. That was how it always shook out. That was where, after one of our break-ups, the talk always led. We'd talk and then we'd fuck and then a few days later he'd move in again, amid a lot of promises and hope. Until the next time.

"Can I come over now? Please, baby."

I felt that creeping hot patch on my neck. The signal of my desire. It didn't much matter what he promised me now, and I was just about to tell him to hurry over, when I was suddenly knocked off my feet by an enormous wave of sadness and guilt. As much for Siggy as for Inge.

"Walter?"

"What, sweetheart?"

"Walter, what would you say was the greatest thing you ever did to earn me?"

"What?"

"You know, the emblematic gesture that said what you want in this world is me."

"What?"

"I mean, I know that you kind of keep me—in a way.

But did you ever do anything to earn me? When was the last time you jumped in front of a bus for me?"

"What the fuck you talking about, Nanette?"

I wasn't listening to Walter anymore. I said I had to hang up. And I did.

I also folded up the newspapers and put them out near the incinerator. I wasn't going to France and I knew it. Not on this sixty grand, anyway.

"Who's there?" Inge called timidly from behind the paint-flecked door to her apartment.

"It's Ann," I responded.

It was dark inside. She closed the door behind me and switched on a lamp.

Inge stood there, blinking every now and again, waiting for me to speak.

"I have something to give you," I said finally.

She cocked her head to the left, but remained silent. Bruno ambled over and took his place at her side.

I reached into my overalls and came out with four of the rolls. "Here."

I pressed them into her hands, swatting away the dog's curious nose.

"What is it?"

"It's money. From Sig. He told me it should go to you if anything ever happened to him. There's . . ." I faltered there, postponing the absurd sentence I was about to pronounce. "There's twenty thousand dollars there, Inge."

"Twenty thousand." She repeated the words as if I were talking about a breakfast cereal.

"That's right. It's not a trick. It's not a joke. Just take it and live your life."

Bruno growled from way down in his chest.

"I told Sig I didn't know if we'd make the rent next month," she said distractedly. "But how did you—"

I ran out of there.

In what had to be the boldest act of my life, out of high compassion and no sense, I had just given away twenty thousand dollars that didn't belong to me—just like that—without thinking.

Which left forty.

So, who was going to be Robin Hood's next have-not?

The old woman in Harlem who rescued the babies with AIDS was dead now, but her work continued. Someone else was operating the charity called Hale House. Perhaps I'd give them something.

What about the United Negro College Fund? What about a yearly stipend for some deserving music student at one of the city colleges?

And there was still that large-breasted, half-bald black girl from Queens who blew tenor on street corners—the one who was so fond of Provence and triple milled soaps. The one who needed to have her head examined at the earliest possible opportunity.

No, none of these, deserving as they might be. It was time for me to come to my senses.

The money—what was left of it—was going where it should have gone five minutes after I'd found it. God help me, I was going to have to turn it over to Leman Sweet.

CHAPTER FIVE

Little Rootie Tootie

The kitchen in the house where I grew up is as pure with light as a day in St. Paul de Vence. And it is invariably spotless. There is an explanation for this: Mom can't cook.

My mother is a child of convenience foods. No homemade cornbread or peach cobbler ever drew breath in that kitchen. We were strictly Colonel Sanders and Mrs. Paul; spinach pie at the Greeks on Metropolitan Avenue, corned beef at the deli in Sunnyside; Sunday trips in to Manhattan for the biscuits at Sylvia's in Harlem or, on a really special occasion, dinner in the theater district before some musical my father was taking us to.

It had nothing to do with my mother's lousy cooking, but Daddy left her about eight years ago. He is a department head at one of those high schools for gifted assholes, and he fell in love with a colleague—a young white teacher nearly half his age. The feeling, apparently, was mutual and so they were wed. Like something out of the Greeks, my mother has not spoken his name since. Mom is going on fifty-five. She is still pretty. I don't look a thing like her.

I placed a roll of bills in the pocket of her mauve shirt-waist with a simple "Happy birthday, Mom."

"Nanette, what is this?"

"It's for you, Mom. Your birthday present."

"Nanette, you already gave me a birthday present—three months ago."

"Right. That was part one. This is part two."

She removed the rubber band from the roll and counted the bills. "Nanette, this is five thousand dollars."

"Yes ma'am, I know."

"Where did this come from?"

"From NYU. It's a bonus."

"Bonus for what?"

"Well, not exactly a bonus. It's more like a prize. For some, uh, books that I translated."

"Well, that's just wonderful. But what would I look like taking your whole fee for that work? You're not supporting me, Nanette."

"It's not my whole fee. It's only half. And I wanted to give it to you now because I'll probably forget your next six birthdays. It's a kind of insurance. And besides, haven't you been talking about repainting the house or something for months now?"

"I want aluminum siding, I said. As if you were listening."

"Well, that's what I mean. It's yours."

In the end she did take the money. After pinning me to the wall with a couple of those patented Mom looks. You know, those looks that can mean anything from *who's going to be wearing pajamas at this pajama party?* to *prison is probably too good for you.* I had seen the full panoply of her looks and now, after nearly thirty years, could all but ignore them.

Mom kissed me and put the bills back in her pocket.

She keeps saying that one day she'll take a vacation someplace nice—maybe even go to Europe. But she never will. She keeps promising to visit me and see my apartment, too, at least to meet me midtown for lunch. But I don't count on that one either. I don't think she even remembers the last time she was in Manhattan.

Mom told me all about aluminum siding. We had tea, Lipton's, which is very hard to get wrong.

She asked after Aubrey, and inquired whether she still had "that beautiful mink jacket that she saved up for" out of her earnings as a restaurant hostess. I knew that her suspicions about what Aubrey really did for a living were probably much worse than the reality. A go go dancer isn't a whore, I wanted to tell her. But it was a little late for that. See, the old folks do have a point—once you tell a lie, you have to go on lying; it just works that way.

A few minutes before it was time for me to go, I went into my old room and called Aubrey. I had to confirm the appointment we'd made. I needed someone there with me when I faced Leman Sweet, and Aubrey had agreed to accompany me; to watch my back, so to speak, since I feared Detective Sweet might get physical again when I told him what I'd done. When I told him even *half* of what I'd done.

"So . . . you really gone do it, huh Nan?" Aubrey asked wearily.

"Yeah, I really am."

"You be better off taking Walter back."

We had taken over a corner of the immense lobby of her

apartment building and fashioned an island of sofas and glass tables and easy chairs. I took a cigarette from Aubrey's pack. As I was striking the match I noticed Leman Sweet swing in through the plate glass doors. As he barreled along, he was being dogged by an irate doorman who had not been responded to in the manner to which he was accustomed. Sweet finally wheeled on the man and flipped open his badge. The doorman removed his hat and wiped his forehead.

"*That's* him?" Aubrey stage whispered to me.

"Oh yeah. That is most definitely him."

"He doesn't look that mean."

She was right.

It was Leman Sweet, all right, but not the same one who had cursed and assaulted me in my own home. He still had the Fu Manchu moustache but he was now dressed in a dark business suit. High-polished Florsheims. Good Presbyterian tie. Good haircut. The quietly competent look. Best of all, he wasn't carrying a musical instrument that might end up smashed to bits against the nearest available surface.

Detective Sweet towered over us like the wish-granting, coal-black genie in my childhood affirmative action story book. I worked up enough courage to meet his eyes.

"Why'd you want to meet here?" he boomed.

"My friend Aubrey lives here," I responded, a clumsy introduction if ever there was one.

But by then Leman had gotten a good look at Aubrey. He went into a kind of moony paralysis. Which was, as Stevie Wonder said, just like I pictured it.

He sat directly across from Aubrey, his legs spread wide, massive thighs outlined in navy blue gabardine, pinky ring flashing—a real prince of the city. "Well, it's a good thing you wanted to meet uptown," he said to me— ostensibly to me—while he was eating Aubrey up, "'cause that's where I was today."

I didn't linger over his non sequitur. No use expecting a smitten man to make sense. Without further ado I merely placed a large, stuffed sweat sock on the little cigarette table in front of him.

"What is that?" he said.

"Money."

"Whose money?"

That's where Aubrey came in, as planned. "Look like it was your friend's," she said. "Officer Conlin. He put it in Nan's sax that night before they killed him."

Sweet, coming reluctantly back to earth, let out a long, low curse.

I allowed Aubrey to go on from there with her narration, describing how, after I'd discovered the money, I was terrified the police—namely Leman—would suspect me of something. How I'd been too scared to report it right away and had come to Aubrey seeking her advice.

At the end of the tale, Sweet took hold of the sock and shook it like a bull terrier with a backyard squirrel. The rolls came tumbling out.

"How much is here?"

"Thirty-five thousand," I spoke up quickly. "About that."

Leman looked at me. My body tensed, preparing for a lunge from him.

"What's the matter, Mr. Sweet?" Aubrey asked and leaned toward him solicitously. "You don't look too happy to find your friend's stash."

"Wasn't *his* stash. Supposed to be the Department's. God-damn, this ain't good," he said solemnly. "Not good at all."

"Why not?"

"There's twenty-five thousand missing."

"Oh my God! Oh, no!" Aubrey said. "What you figure happened to it, Mr. Sweet?"

Aubrey, crossing and uncrossing her legs, lighting his Newports, playing first the bumpkin and then the slut, got the story out of Leman Sweet. He told us about the failed undercover operation he and Charlie Conlin had been working on: It seems "the Dominicans" were starting to use street musicians and flower vendors to retail stolen tokens, money orders, passports and even lottery tickets. He and Conlin/Sig had been part of a huge sting that had gone bust. The fortune that Conlin left in my sax case was so-called buy money. And Leman didn't know why Charlie had been carrying it around.

We all sat in silence for a few moments. Then Aubrey laughed obscenely. "Look like your partner was deep into something, Sweet."

He nodded.

"But you know," she continued, "a fella like that coulda spent sixty thousand just as quick as he spent that missing twenty-five. Your department probably figure the whole sixty already gone, right, Sweet? Right? I mean, ain't they already kissed it good-bye, Sweet?"

He said nothing, just twisted the sock until the contents were secure, and then pocketed it. Sweet leaned back into the sofa and lit another Newport, holding on to the paper match long after its flame had died.

I looked at him while he drooled. I looked at Aubrey

looking at him. What a nasty little dance. It would lead nowhere, of course.

I had an absurd vision of Leman Sweet in a tight-fitting French navy uniform, walking all lovey-dovey with Aubrey through Marseilles. Then I cast myself in the female role, hanging onto his arm while I chatted over my shoulder with the odd fishmonger about the novels of Marcel Pagnol. It was almost enough to make me pull out my notebook and dash off a few lines. Needless to say, that poem would have been squarely in the surrealist tradition.

All that aside, I could feel my chest expanding with the sweet rush of a righteous act. I had done what I was supposed to do—give back that money. It may have been a little short, it may have been a little late, but I'd done it! Sweet seemed to buy our version of events. And Sig—in all his incarnations—would be out of my life forever.

Thank the baby Jesus, Leman Sweet left us at last.

Aubrey leaned forward and consulted the mirrored top of the little cigarette table. She freshened her lipstick, all the while shaking her head in bemused contempt.

"What?" I asked.

"Country nigger," she said low. "Where the fuck he get off hittin' you?"

CHAPTER SIX

Misterioso

I stopped dreaming about Leman Sweet and his thunder thighs and his fists like dressed pork roasts. Stopped fearing that he was going to come and beat me up every time I watched TV instead of running scales on the horn; every time I said an unkind word about anyone or failed to sort the recyclables or ignored a phone message.

I threw away the Marseilles pimp poem.

Mom had an appointment with the rip-off contractors who do shit like aluminum siding. They were going to give her an estimate.

And, oh yeah: Walt and I reconciled, in the usual way. The sex was still excellent. And he was for the most part on his best behavior—the upswing of the getting-back-together arc: dinners at those little places where he would take a client he was wooing; a fifty here and there to tide me over; always the movie *I* wanted to see.

He was empathy itself when I recounted the horror story about Sig being murdered in my place, palpably guilty that he hadn't been around to help me, suitably outraged over my treatment at the hands of the police. He did get a bit obnoxious with his jealous insistence on knowing what this long-haired white man was doing in my apartment in the first place. But I managed to make him feel like a petty lowlife for thinking about his dick when my very life had been at stake.

So the sheets were humming and the Con Ed bill was paid. Walt and I were back on solid ground.

Except he didn't move back in this time. He didn't ask. I didn't invite. Despite the good times, there was still a diamond hard core of mistrust between us. I regretted that, wished it weren't true, but there it was. He knew my moods and he knew my body, just as I did his, but there was that vast campground of head and heart where we almost never met. Once again I knew the pleasures of that fevered stripping off of clothes and Walter's gorgeous chest and all the lovely wet stuff, the glass of cold wine and one of his cigarettes just before sleep and the so-long kiss the next morning. But I guess I'm just some kind of pervert when you get right down to it. It seemed I was genuinely happy only when I could nail him on some crap he was trying to pull.

But while my love life had its limitations, my "professional" life was no less than blossoming . . . leaping . . . pumping . . . hot. A highly respected musician who had made a good living in the New York music world for some forty years—a friend of a friend—had accepted me as a student. We were going to start working together in a month or so. Was I excited? No. I was more than excited— I was serious. Practicing my ass off. For the first time in years, I was serious about something other than finding a bargain on red wine.

As a kind of homage to Sig, I kept to that same spot just off Thirty-fourth and Lexington, even though he had told me I could make more money west. After all, while I really was applying myself to my music, I realized, number one, that I was at heart a novelty act—a big girl with long legs and a bald head—and number two, most of the people playing for coins west of Fifth Avenue would have blown me off the sidewalk.

So what if I wasn't ready to play "Body and Soul"? I had my fans nonetheless. The tips in my hat were showing a steady increase, a few fives among the singles. And then, one day, somebody gave me something a lot more thrilling than five bucks.

I was blowing something playful—a 1950s thing called "The Late Show"—pretending that Dakota Staton was singing in my left ear—when I saw a strange-looking shadow fall across the pavement. The shape turned out to be a young kid with a bouquet of flowers in his arms. I finished the set and bent to gather up my take. The boy went on standing there, smiling. Then he thrust the wrapped flowers into my hand.

"This is for me?"

"Yeah. With a note," he said.

I pointed down to my hat. He scooped up two quarters as his tip and was gone.

I undid the wrapping paper.

God! Long-stemmed yellow roses. Nine of them. All perfect. A creamy yellow note card too, but nothing written on it. Instead, a twenty-dollar bill paperclipped to it.

I looked around in wonderment. I looked up to all the buildings where someone could be standing behind a curtain, pining for me. I looked down the avenue and around the corner and at every doorway. It was such a crazy thing, getting those flowers, so moving and yet so weird, that instead of breaking for lunch I packed up my sax and went home.

The piece I wrote that night about the incident had the nine roses turning into eighteen, and the eighteen into thirty-six, and so on. Multiplying, dividing, transmutating. You know . . . roses, rose hips, my hips, hips, lips, yellow so yellow it's white hot, its intensity like the sewing needle my mother once used to take a splinter out of my heel.

Next day, it happened again. Only the delivery boy was different. And as for the new batch of roses—those lovesome things—they were younger, a trifle smaller, their heads tightly curled back onto themselves and sitting atop pale green leaf collars—the yellow was even deeper. Impossibly deep, hypnotical yellow. I wanted to eat one. Could all but feel that color dripping down the side of my mouth like egg.

I finished out the afternoon, which, without my noticing, had turned to velvet. Blew nothing but ballads. Two hip-looking dykes asked for an encore of "Don't Blame Me." Finished with "Violets for My Fur." Sixty-two big ones in the fedora. *Ran* home. Found second vase. Unplugged phone. Threw *Lady Day* on the machine. Poured drink. Long bath. No supper. Masturbated. Slept like top.

I decided to clean up my act a little the next day. I put on Monk's all-Ellington album while I pressed a skirt lightly and scared up a clean shirt and made coffee and picked up a little around the apartment. Then dressed and hunted for that Indian fabric out of which I had fashioned a neck strap for the ax. Finally I was ready to leave the house. I'd walked half a block before I realized my telephone was still unplugged. I ran back and reconnected it and the answering machine, and, as long as I was there, put on a pair of earrings.

That was the day I caught him.

I arrived at the corner at an off time, about an hour later than usual. The flowers came right away. And across the street I saw a man watching the delivery. He was standing in the recessed doorway of a run-down apartment building, looking highly furtive. He had a Mediterranean aura—maybe he was Greek, or Lebanese . . . Israeli? No. Whatever he was, he looked pretty unhappy in his expensive black overcoat and silk scarf. He was smoking furiously.

I watched him for a few minutes, waiting for him to make a move. But he stood his ground, lighting one cigarette after another. Well, maybe I was mistaken. Maybe he wasn't my secret admirer. I set up and started to play.

I saluted the newborn season, starting with "Autumn in New York." Then "Autumn Nocturne," during which my old friend, the one-armed gambler, strolled by, tossing a few coins in the hat with an apologetic shrug. Then "Autumn Serenade." I was just about to play "Lullaby of the Leaves" when the rose man crossed the street.

He took a few steps toward me, but then immediately backed away. I raised the sax to my lips and once again he stepped forward, this time muttering to himself. What the hell was the matter with this guy? When he was quite close, I pointed down at the bouquet and smiled at him. It was a question.

He nodded, reluctantly at first, and then more vigorously.

"Who are you?"

"My name is Henry Valokus," he said with a half bow.

"And I am embarrassed at what I have done." He didn't have an accent, exactly, but he spoke English in this queer, slow way—with a kind of all-purpose, assimilated European lilt.

"What have you done, Henry?"

"The flowers."

"But they're exquisite. They don't embarrass me."

"I have listened to you since you first came here. Listened to your playing. You are charming."

Now I was a bit embarrassed.

"You've sent so many roses. I've run out of vases, you know."

"Ah," he said, "then I have done too much. I always do too much. It is my nature."

He stood there smiling shyly at me while I memorized his face. Every crag and culvert of it. And especially those black mourning eyes.

"I would consider it a great honor if you would lunch with me."

I hesitated.

"For instance," he went on, "we might go to one of the nearby Indian restaurants here on Lexington."

Mr. Henry Valokus had pushed the right button. I love Indian food desperately. There was a time there, twelve or thirteen pounds ago, when I was eating it for breakfast.

"You have finished?"

I wondered if he was being sarcastic. I wasn't just finished, I was bursting. "Oh, believe me," I said, "I am finished."

He signalled the waiter and removed a silver cigarette case from his breast pocket in a single, fluid motion.

"It must be difficult to make a living as you do," he said sympathetically. "I wanted to make things nice for you."

I laughed and took one of the proffered cigarettes without even looking at the brand. "What a *gallant* you are, Henry. Do you make a practice of rescuing penurious lady musicians? Or am I special?"

"You are special," he answered immediately.

I let that one lay there for a few minutes. I blew across the top of my spiced tea to help it cool.

I hadn't even noticed him order the drinks, but a few minutes later two outsized snifters were placed before us.

"You appreciate cognac," Henry stated. "I am certain I have not guessed wrong about that."

"Henry, you have yet to hit a wrong note. But listen . . ."

He leaned in close.

". . . What, exactly, are you after?"

Mr. Valokus's face went a little red. After a minute, he said, "I will be totally honest with you."

"Okay. Honest is good."

"What I would like from you is . . . is . . . to . . . well, to understand."

"Understand what?"

"Music. Well, not all music. One particular thing, I mean. Something—someone—that is with me like a ghost, like a memory. Except that I don't understand where it came from."

"Henry, you've lost me."

"Let me say it this way: if you were to come with me to my apartment at this moment—"

I burst into a guffaw, but when I saw the hurt on his face I stopped laughing. With a nod of my head I signalled that he should continue.

"If you were to come to my apartment, what you would find is a kind of shrine I have created. Hundreds of recordings. Hundreds, I tell you. And books. And photographs. Posters. Posters everywhere. And all concerning a single musician. The one who obsesses me. And until I have a complete understanding of him and his music, until I have comprehended his heart and his soul, he will obsess me. As long as I live. Do you see, Nanette, what I am saying?"

"Not at all," I said. "But who's the musician?"

"Bird."

"Beg pardon?"

"Parker."

"As in Charlie?"

"Yes. Of course."

"You're telling me you're obsessed with Charlie Parker?"

"Yes. It is true."

"And you want me to help you *understand*?"

He nodded.

This time I couldn't hold it back. Before long, I was doubled over with laughter. Racism is a stitch, ain't it? White people think you're either a half wit, genetically determined criminal or an extraterrestrial with some kind of pipeline to *the spirit*.

Oh well. There didn't seem to be much point in going out on this weird guy, Valokus, whose face had again clouded over with pain and incomprehension. Besides, what was he asking of me, essentially? To talk to him about music. What was so bad about that? It wasn't as though he was asking me to clean his place or suck his dick.

So I pulled myself together and took another sip of my

cognac. Charlie Parker wasn't no goddamn mystic, he was a musical genius—for some, *the* musical genius—fucked up behind heroin and being an American Negro—so what else is new? But instead of saying that to Henry, I reached over and patted his hand a little.

In turn, he took mine and kissed it lingeringly. Then he called for the bottle of Remy and poured me a really big drink.

Valokus took me back to my corner and left me there with the paper container of cappuccino he had purchased at the new café in the neighborhood. He was going uptown now, he said, because he'd heard Colony Records had a new shipment of some live recordings of Bird club dates.

Just the tiniest bit unsteady on my feet, I watched him walk up the block and disappear around the corner.

Pity I'm not a true whore, I thought. I could take this fool for a real ride.

Henry wasn't kidding. His apartment, which I visited after our third lunch date, was a shrine to Charlie Parker.

Everywhere you looked there was a piece of Bird memorabilia: poster-size blow-ups of old black and white photos of Parker, "Bird Lives" calendars, back issue jazz magazines, an unpublished PhD thesis, books, postcards.

And then there was the music itself: records, cassettes, CDs.

I was speechless. This time it didn't occur to me to laugh at Henry's Birdmania. Something happened on that first visit to his shrine that made me a little less high handed about his obsession. A sudden shock of recognition, I guess. I realized that my feeling for France may not have been so different from Henry's Birdaholism.

France was hardly my home. Yet I kept fleeing there. It was where I felt safe, the most alive, the most understood, the most welcome. French was not my mother tongue. Yet if I had my way every school child would start studying it at age six. I tried to write in that language. I loved the way it felt in my mouth. I was positively turned on just hearing it on the radio. But that was all romantic crap. I'm not French. And no power on earth could make it otherwise. I'm as colored and American as Charlie Parker. That moment of recognition and empathy with Henry Valokus was a turning point in my attitude toward him. His Bird thing was no longer just silly; it had become endearing.

We talked quite animatedly that afternoon about our shared disappointment with the film they'd made about Parker's life, though we both loved the actors who'd played Bird and Chan. We chose five tunes and dug through all the music in the apartment, comparing live versions of those songs to studio-recorded ones; early recordings to late ones; those done in New York to those recorded in Boston to those recorded in California. Before long we were hungry again. Henry ordered in Indian food from a grand place on Fifty-sixth Street and champagne from the liquor store and the talk fest continued.

It wasn't until he'd closed the cab door after me that night and the driver pulled away from the curb that it occurred to me: Henry had not tried to make me. Not once.

So, after dinner a few days later, I seduced him.

On the elevator up to his place, I wanted him so much I thought I was going to detonate. The wanting was like a noose around my neck. But I was cool. And remained so through both sides of the *Parker with Strings* cassette we'd picked up from a street vendor in the Village. I was wearing the world's shortest suede skirt, absolutely sure I was sending out telegrams of sexual funk, and pretty sure he was answering the door. He put on the smokiest ballads in the house, and while I sat eating a seckle pear, he took off his tie. Then, out of the blue, he asked me to dance with him!

Which I did, for about sixty seconds, just long enough for the first extended kiss. And then I knocked him down.

His mouth on my nipple sent chain lightning through me. As he rolled down my tights and began to stroke me I gripped him, scratched him, as if I were trying to mark him for my own. I came and came back again, came and came back again. I tore him out of his pants there in the lamplight and took *him*. We fucked on top of a Nat Hentoff essay. We did it standing up under a framed photo of the Birdland marquee. I couldn't get enough of him, couldn't feel enough of him inside me—thick, strange, hungry. And when he had no more to give me, when he was lost in his own frantic shivering, I opened my mouth mercilessly and bit into him like a cannibal.

CHAPTER SEVEN
Trinkle Tinkle

 I had two lovers. Two men do not a slut make. But, still and all, two ain't one.

Aubrey thought it was funny.

Walter didn't.

No, I didn't tell him. I didn't have to. He noticed.

He had just come out of the shower that morning. I was making coffee. By the time he was dressed for work, Walter had turned sullen. He took a seat across from me in the kitchen, ignoring the plate in front of him.

"Just so you don't think you're getting away with something, Nan, I know you're fucking around."

I didn't answer.

"Skeevy bitch."

"Cut it out, Walter."

"Cut what out? You're dogging around and you know it."

"Walter, you sound like a tired housewife. I'm not your goddamn property. You never slept with anybody else while we were together?"

Things took the predictable elevator up from there, ending with his wordless, self-righteous departure for the office. He didn't slam the front door. Matter of fact, he didn't even bother to close it.

I sat alone for a while, feeling tired and torn—and guilty—until I decided I'd better hit the streets and make some money.

It was hard to shake the bad mood. After an hour of playing I repaired to a busy coffee place on Thirty-fourth Street. The jelly donuts were tops, and I needed a shot of sugar, bad. The guy sitting next to me finished his chocolate croissant (I had tried one once—too oily) and walked out. I picked up the *Daily News* he'd left behind and started flipping through it.

Page three was where I stopped flipping.

BRAVE POOCH DIES
DEFENDING BLIND MISTRESS

One of the grainy photos accompanying the story showed a hulking, lifeless animal lying on its side. "Seeing eye dog and mistress both stabbed to death" was the caption. Next to that was a picture of a young woman three-quarters covered by an EMS blanket.

"Fuck," I said aloud.

It was Inge—Mrs. Sig, the musician. And that graceless seeing eye dog of hers—Bruno.

I forced myself to read on. The young woman and her dog, the article said, were both dead when police arrived on the scene. She has been identified as Inge Carlson. No witnesses had, as yet, come forward. Police said the motive for the killings was not known, but of course they had not ruled out the possibility that the girl and her canine companion had walked in on a robbery in progress.

I stared dumbly at the photo of that silly dog. Somehow I couldn't bring myself to look at Inge's face again. I wondered if her sightless eyes shone any brighter in death, but I was too scared to look, too sickened.

In my dumbass attempts to do right, I'd managed to cut a pretty wide swath through the endless possibilities of wrong. Sig, the undercover cop I'd taken in off the street, was dead because I'd made him sleep in the other room.

As for Walter, we'd been through the best and the worst together. I gladly took his money when I needed it, and his time, and his sex, and even, once in a while, his advice. In his own weird way, he loved me, I think. But I was fucking around on him, just as he'd said. Even if I was genuinely in love with the eccentric and gallant Henry Valokus—and I was—I was still cuckolding old Walt.

And now this, the latest grotesquerie. There was no doubt in my mind that the blind girl and her dog were dead because of that twenty thousand dollars I'd given her—her inheritance from Sig. I thought I was doing the right thing, the compassionate thing, the correct thing. Following the gospel according to Ernestine.

"Fuck!" I kept repeating through the tears I fought to keep in my throat.

There was a phone in the back of the coffee shop. I fumbled through my wallet and found Leman Sweet's card.

I left my name and the number of the coffee shop pay-phone on his voice mail. "It's urgent," I added. Then I took a seat near the phone and waited.

It took about twenty minutes for him to call back.

"What can I do for you?" he began, grudgingly civil. I guess I was still riding for free on his feelings for Aubrey.

"I just read the paper," I said. "Do you have anything to do with that blind girl thing? The one who was murdered?"

Sweet didn't answer for a minute.

"What's that to you?" he finally said.

"Do you?"

"You figure it out, college girl. You saw me with the fucking guitar. I explained the undercover gig to you, with the street musicians. She was a street musician. I was supposed to be a street musician. What do you think?"

"The paper didn't say anything about the musician angle."

"Paper didn't say a lot of things. How dumb are you?"

Actually, I could have answered that one. But I refrained. This was no time for self-pity.

"Hello?"

"I'm still here," I said.

"What's this all about, college? Do you know something about that chick?"

"Yeah."

"What have you done, girl?"

"I gave her twenty thousand dollars—the money that was missing from Charlie Conlin's socks."

"Fuck."

"Yeah, I know."

"Are you saying you been in that apartment where she was killed?"

"Yeah. That's what I'm saying."

"Where are you?" he boomed into the receiver.

* * *

I'd used up every bit of the goodwill Aubrey had built for me with Leman Sweet. He was back to hating me. But I'd made up my mind that if he so much as breathed on me this time I was going to pick up a bottle and kill him with it.

I was waiting on the street when he pulled up to the coffee shop in his standard issue, plain clothes car. He reached over and opened the passenger door, barely looking at me.

"Since you like to meddle with police business so much, I'm taking you to the scene of the crime," he said when I'd slammed the door closed.

I had deliberately placed the sax case between us on the front seat. I kept my eyes fixed on the busy streets, on the people walking free, living, happy—not trapped like me, not hurtling toward some dark unknown, like me.

"Start talking," Sweet commanded.

"What do you want me to say?"

"How did you know Inge Carlson?"

"I didn't know her. I found her."

"How?"

"I asked around the street. Sig—I mean Conlin—had told me about her."

"And where did you get the bright idea to give away twenty grand of New York City Police money to a blind whore?"

"I didn't know it was your money, Mr. Sweet. I figured Conlin got it from someplace pretty bad, that he'd done whatever he had to do to get it, but it was his. If she was his lady, then some of it should go to her. Any kind of a man would want that."

Sweet's mouth pulled back unattractively from his big teeth. "I wonder," he said, "if you learned your line of bullshit in school or whether you're just a born liar."

"I'm not lying."

"Yeah, sure. And that blind girl ain't dead."

One good thing had happened: Sweet's power over me—his ability to terrify me—was dwindling rapidly. His contempt and scorn were fast becoming a bore.

"Okay," I said quietly. "I'm the world's biggest liar. Let's move on to something else. Why are you taking me to her apartment?"

"I want you to show me exactly what happened when you gave that money away."

"Nothing 'happened.' I just gave it to her."

"There's a potential witness been turned up too. I want him to take a look at you. A good look."

"Just in case I gave her the money and then came back and stole it from her—and then killed her—right?"

"You irritate the shit outta me, you know that?"

"I'd gathered."

"We gonna see how smart you are later, when I take your ass to the station . . . little miss genius."

I sat back and sighed heavily, wondering whether Leman had washed out of junior college somewhere.

Inge's place looked almost the same. Almost. Except now it had that low-level, greasy glare a room takes on when something awful has happened there. Like my place the night Charlie Conlin was killed. And, like my home that night, her place had become utterly unprivate. Strange people—cops—coming and going at will. Poking at things, being careless with their cigarettes, talking too loud.

A policewoman looked over at Sweet. "Ready?" she asked.

"Yeah. Send him in."

She hurried off. A slight young man no more than twenty with dark hair walked in a minute later. Eyes downcast, he stood next to the half-opened door, reluctant to enter the room. He might have been Latino, or Hawaiian, or Filipino. I couldn't get a clear look at his face. The boy's hair was cut very short and on one side of his scalp a pair of initials were incised. His big shirt and ballooning, low riding jeans completed the pathetic picture of a kid lamely trying to carry off the b-boy thing. Somebody should break it to him, I thought, that the happening look is now running to button down shirts and Hush Puppies.

"Hey!"

Leman Sweet's ogre-like baritone snapped the kid to attention. He looked at Sweet and seemed to shiver.

"Your name's Diego, right?" Sweet demanded.

He nodded.

"Take a look at her." He meant me. "Take a good look."

Diego stared at me, uncomprehending. I looked back into his dark, frightened eyes.

"You ever see her before?"

"No."

I didn't bother to glance Sweet's way. I merely took a seat at the kitchen table while he began to question the boy who, he said, was born in the Dominican Republic.

"You told the officer you heard something going on in here the day the blind girl was murdered."

"They killed her dog, too, didn't they?"

"That's right."

"I liked that dog. She used to let him come in the shop sometime. Sometime I give him a bone to—"

Sweet cut him off. "What did you hear that day?"

"Music."

"What kind of music?"

"I don't know."

"What do you mean, you don't know? It was her playing the sax, wasn't it?"

"No," he said defiantly. "Not that. I'm not talking about that. This was a man's voice, singing. Like he was here singing to her. It could have been a tape, I guess."

"Ain't nothing in here to play a tape on, man."

"Well, maybe the radio. But I don't think so. It didn't sound like that."

"What did it sound like?"

"I told you, I don't know! It coulda been that country stuff."

"Country—you mean that C&W shit—like *red neck, white socks, and Blue Ribbon Beer?*"

Diego didn't get it.

"Why don't you just tell me what you heard," Sweet said.

"He said his eyes was red from the road."

"Come again?"

"His eyes are red in the song. He said something about the road and eyes lined red. It didn't sound like any music I heard before—more like just talking. Except his voice was loud. And he kept saying it over. 'Road ... eyes ... lined ... red ... road ... eyes ... lined ... red.' It wasn't like the way people talk, man. It was like a song."

"Shit, you telling me somebody was in here singing a stupidass truckers' lullaby to that woman before they offed her?"

Again, Diego seemed to be having trouble following the thread of Leman's questions. I wondered if it had occurred to Sweet, as it just had to me, that Diego was a little stoned. Great. Just the complicating factor we needed.

Sweet kept at it with the boy, but it was no good. The kid had not seen who was "singing" to Inge. Finally he was allowed to return to his work downstairs in the flower market.

Not me. Sweet was as good as his word. He dragged me to the station house, where I was questioned and deposed and warned and 'buked and scorned, whatever that means.

By the time Sweet released me, I was so tired I wasn't sure if I could stand on my feet and walk home. I got as far as the corner of the block where the station house was located before I broke down. I lay the sax in its case against the side of a building and cried for about ten minutes. Nobody bothered me.

Then I dried my eyes, walked over to the payphone, and called Henry. My words came out in a torrent of fear and sorrow. I was telling the story this way and that, all out of order—Inge and the dog and Wild Bill and Sig and Kurt Weill and yellow roses and Leman Sweet.

He listened patiently and then, rather than trying to parse it out there, told me to wait at the phone booth, that he was coming to pick me up.

No, I said, No. I had to get out of there. I couldn't stand the thought of running into Leman Sweet again. I just wanted to get home.

Good idea, said Henry, almost as if he were speaking to a mental patient. And I couldn't blame him, really. I must've been hysterical. Go home directly, Nanette, he instructed. I'll meet you there—All right, darling?

My place is quite a switch from Henry's high-rise love nest. From the landing, I watched him as he climbed the stairs, each step bringing his mournful, befuddled little face into sharper focus.

"Are you all right?" he said, arms out.

I opened my mouth to answer, but nothing much came out. "Oh," was all I could say, "Oh, O'Rooney." I had taken to calling him by the nonsensical name that singer Slim Gaillard had invented for Charlie Parker during an impromptu recording session.

"Come inside, love. Let me see you."

He sat me down at the kitchen table while he made a pot of tea for me. I drank it slowly, gradually calming down, and finally was able to relate the story coherently.

"Henry," I said mournfully, "what am I going to do? I got her killed. I got her *killed*, Henry."

"But you did not, Nan. How could you know what would happen? You were only trying to give help to a blind girl. She said she couldn't even pay her rent."

"I know, but, Christ! It's so awful. I'm like a wrecking crew, Rooney. Everything I touch seems to crumble and die. Maybe you better beat it back to that loft you once had on the rue Dauphine. I don't think my tentacles can reach as far as Paris."

"I pay no attention when you say such things, Nanette."

In each pocket of Henry's overcoat was a brown paper bag. The bags contained identical bottles of cheap Chilean wine which he had picked up, no doubt, at the benighted little liquor store up the block.

He poured me a glass and undid the buttons of my blouse as I drank. "Go and change your things now," he said. "I will make something to eat."

I don't know what kind of mouldering condiments Henry found in the fridge or the cabinets, but with their help he made me some fantastic scrambled eggs. I ate like a wolf. We found some stale Fig Newtons in the cabinet and I devoured those too, along with half a quart of milk.

"You were hungry, yes?" he said, smiling. "The way you were when you came in from school and your mother gave you those . . . those biscuits."

"Yes!" In my mind I saw, clear as a bell, the image of Mom in her pristine apron. "Milk Lunch Biscuits. She thought they were a treat. But I hated them. My mother never did understand about food."

"Mine did, of course. You are lucky you did not have her as a mother. You would have been a very fat little child indeed."

"But you weren't. You were skinny. And a mama's boy. And *everything* was fried in olive oil."

"You remember everything I tell you about my childhood, and I remember all about yours," Henry remarked. "Our lives could not have been more different. And yet, I feel as if I lived there alongside you in Elmhurst. And as if you swam with me and ate the same sweet things as me in my grandmother's kitchen."

"Me too," I said. "I guess we've touched souls, Henry. That's what all the poems are about."

"I want to see some of your poetry."

I rolled my eyes. "Oh, God. Maybe another night, sweetie."

"You used to write them in school. When you were so unhappy. When you were daydreaming."

"I could have used a friend like you in school."

He smiled slyly. "Do not be so sure. The only way I could have known you then is if I were your teacher. I might have kept you long, long after school—touching souls with you. And then what would your parents think?"

We both laughed.

"Do you know what I am thinking of now?" he asked mischievously as we cleared the dishes.

"What?"

"That strange hotel near the Opera, off the boulevard Haussmann, where I had the flu."

"Yes. The hotel du Nil. Where all the maids were from Barbados."

"I stayed there when I was very young. And so did you. And we both thought that *nil* meant zero, when it really meant the Nile River. What do you think that means, Nanette, that we both made the same mistake?"

"I don't know. But did your mom also tell you when you were little that you were a very smart child, but sometimes you were a fool too?"

"Maybe. I suspect not. In fact, I don't think anyone has ever told me I was very smart."

I took the dish towel from him and kissed his hands. "That's all right, Rooney. You're smart enough for me."

"At any rate," he added, "I never stayed in that hotel again—or anywhere in the ninth. I found it much more romantic to live in the sixth, or in Montmartre. Before the long walk back to my room, I would drink a brandy every night at the Café Maroc because it was where all the performers went. And the shady characters."

"Did you get yourself seduced by any female tightrope walkers?"

"Never."

"Lady saxophonists?"

"No. You are my first. Take your things off, please," Henry requested humbly.

I had never been made love to more sweetly than that night. Nor will I ever be again, most likely.

We undressed in the living room and lay in each other's arms on the floor. No more talking for a long while. I was desolate, lost, when it was finished, until he covered me once more with his body and placed his hands on my face and kissed me until I was happy again.

The city had grown dark, black.

"If you will not recite your poetry tonight," he told me, "I insist that you play something for me."

I shrugged. "Okay."

I dragged my sax out and stood in the center of the room, naked, inspired by all that was in my heart. I chose Ellington's "Daydream," making believe I was Johnny Hodges.

There was one more glassful left in the bottle. I poured it out and we shared it while we listened to the sides Parker had recorded with a mixed chorus. Henry bathed and shampooed me to the innocuous strains of "Old Folks."

Inge Carlson. That was her name. Charlie Conlin. That was his. Both murdered. Two white people, two strangers, had flashed in and flashed out of my life and maybe changed it forever. The road to forgetting them and the way they died seemed to stretch out ahead of me like some terrible highway. I might be old before I forgot. But I had Henry to thank for starting me on that path.

I figured I'd sleep till next summer. But after Henry was gone, my eyes popped right open again—mind racing, fear and weariness tapping on my bones. I gave up and got out

of bed. I went into the kitchen and poured myself a slug of
the Martel Cordon Supreme I'd brought back from France
two years ago and had jealously guarded since then.

Why me? That age-old question.

Why did Sig have to die in *my* kitchen?

Why did my good-intentioned gift of that money to
pretty, sightless Inge have to end up in her murder? And
her poor dog! Who would do that?

There were some awfully bad people about. And I felt
like one of them.

I had another drink.

I reached for the pad of white notepaper that I kept on
the counter, near the telephone. I wanted to write something for Inge. For a few moments, absolutely nothing
came. And then one of Rimbaud's lines started to intrude:

> *During my bitter hours I conjure up sapphire
> hailstones.*

This surely was a bitter hour. It was hard to put words to
what I was feeling, and so I just drew lines, lines and cir-
cles and triangles intersecting. There was nothing in me.
All I could write down were those strange words that the
Dominican kid had heard, or thought he heard. The words
the killer had shouted . . . or sung.

A road.

Eyes lined red.

Red lined eyes.

What had Leman Sweet called it? A stupidass truckers'
lullaby. Blues for rednecks.

I copied the phrases over and over: Road. Eyes. Lined.
Red.

I wrote them on the page horizontally, vertically.

Road. Eyes. Lined. Red.

Road

Eyes

Lined

Red

ROADEYESLINEDRED

I found myself giggling suddenly. If you said it really fast it sounded like—like "Rhode Island Red." A rooster? A hen?

I'd heard of Baltimore Oriole—that was by Hoagy Carmichael, I thought, or maybe it was Johnny Mercer. There was a mockingbird on a hill. There was a yellow bird in a banana tree. A rooster who crowed at the break of dawn. A snowbird, a bluebird, a yardbird, a flamingo. But, as far as I knew, nobody had ever written about a Rhode Island Red.

Rhode Island Red. That's what the bastard said to Inge before he took her life? No, that was crazy. Or I was.

I stoppered the cut glass brandy bottle.

On another sheet of paper I drew a crude, outsized chicken, its mouth gaping open, eyes bugged. The bulging eyes and the twisted mouth, as Billie Holiday had described the body of a lynching victim. I stared at the terrible drawing as I finished my last drink.

I had to do something about all the havoc I'd caused. I had to. Ernestine was popping up everywhere in the kitchen—accusing me, chastising me. And she was right. But I wanted to shout back at her that if she hadn't bugged me to get Sig's money to his lady, Inge might still be alive.

A plan came to me. I would start with that mean old Negro, Wild Bill. I was going to go to him again and talk to him about Inge. Yes, if I woke up tomorrow, and looked at these insane scribblings and could remember what had happened today, that was what I was going to do.

I took a final look at the slips of white paper strewn over the kitchen table. I would crack up soon if I didn't stop this nonsense.

The weariness overtook me then, and the need to sleep. I staggered back to my bed.

CHAPTER EIGHT

Criss-Cross

 I didn't get out of bed till 10 A.M. I felt like I weighed three hundred pounds. Plus, I was good and hung.

Taking a pee, I sat looking at the crazy bird I had drawn last night. Drinking super strong coffee, I read the words Rhode Island Red over and over.

It didn't make sense. But on the other hand, it didn't make no sense. So the decision was sealed. I was going to look up my man Wild Bill.

Henry called while I was dressing. I said no to his lunch invitation and told him I'd probably be tied up all afternoon looking for the cantankerous Wild Bill.

"You should not, you know. Your heart is so generous," he said, "but perhaps you too do not know when to stop." Henry was worried about me.

"I'm cool, Henry. Nothing to it. You just be a good little sex god and I'll tell you how to order the tape of a radio interview with you-know-who's wife."

"You mean Rebecca Parker is still alive?"

"That's right, Henry O'Rooney."

"Be careful, Nan."

So lightning struck twice. My best beau was only a block away from the spot where I'd first found him, just south and west of Penn Station. I hung back while he tried to blow some Art Farmer changes on "Funny Valentine," but he was nowhere near it. He was sweating a little in his tan suit and robin red vest. If I had to guess, I'd say Wild Bill needed a drink. After a while, he gave up and pulled a mouth harp out of his pants pocket. Playing that didn't seem to tax him so much. He did some standard blues riffs. Not bad, but Muddy Waters he wasn't.

The quarters clinked into his case as the noon crowd shuffled along. I looked down at Wild Bill's feet and saw that he was wearing red patent leather shoes—a Salvation Army loss leader, no doubt—and for a minute my heart softened toward him.

"Aw, shit . . . If it ain't old Salt Peanuts again."

He was talking to me, of course.

"How's it going, Mr. Bill?" I folded a dollar and dropped it in his case.

He made a faintly lewd sound back in his throat.

"Let me ask you something," I said. "You read the papers much?"

He startled me then, raising the harmonica to his lips and blasting me back with a tuneless fanfare.

"Inge is dead. She was murdered the other day," I shouted viciously.

He didn't respond at all, not at first. Then he lifted up his nappy head and sang scratchily, directly into my face, "Flat Foot Floogie with the Floy Floy."

Wild Bill was a hard guy to love. I had tried my best to have a little sympathy for him. Who knew why he was so bloody to me—maybe I looked like his ex-wife or something. "Do you remember the other day, when I asked you—"

"I remember you the mailman," he interrupted, "but you ain't brought no news I want to hear."

That deriding laugh of his drove me crazy. I knew I wouldn't be able to take a great deal more from him, so I asked simply, "What do you know about Rhode Island Red?"

No comeback. No nothing. Without saying another word, Wild Bill gathered his stuff and turned on his heel.

"Hey!" I called out when he stepped into the Eighth Avenue traffic.

That old guy really picked up his feet then. I ran to the uptown corner, trying to catch the light before it changed, trying to cut him off before he could head into the train station.

I couldn't. I caught sight of his stained suit jacket just as he disappeared into the tunnel leading to the IRT. By the time I'd fought my way through the milling knot of commuters and homeless and pickpockets and cops, Wild Bill was gone. I knew finding him a third time was not going to be the basic falling off a log that encounters one and two had been.

I knew something else: The word combination I'd come up with—Rhode Island Red—couldn't be very far off the money. And it was obviously something more than a tune that never made it out of Tin Pan Alley.

Roots do tell, don't they? Middle class is middle class. I was stumped, a little frightened, and really depressed. And so I went shopping. At Macy's.

*   *   *

I bought a good black wool sweater on the fourth floor and some divine Parma ham in The Cellar. I had walked home, made lunch, put on coffee, even listened to all my messages before it occurred to me what today was. I ran to the radio and locked in KCR. I had utterly forgotten Thelonious Monk's birthday. Come October 10, I usually do everything short of baking a three-layer cake to celebrate that man's birth. But it had slipped my mind this time. Damn. WKCR each year holds a twenty-four-hour marathon during which they play Monk exclusively. That, along with the April 7 Lady Day salute, is the signal reason I've been sending in my yearly twenty-buck donation to the station since I was old enough to vote.

The announcer reeled off all the great stuff I'd missed just in the previous half hour alone. I was plenty pissed, but I took consolation in the thought that I had the next ten hours or so to lose myself—and some of my troubles—in the music.

Then the phone rang.

Against my better judgment, I answered it. It was Earl, the barkeep at the Emporium, the joint where Aubrey worked. He said she was working the early shift today and needed me to stop by late in the afternoon.

I knew what it was about.

Aubrey was a great deal more solvent than I ever hoped to be. She was a great deal more enterprising too, but I never knew the exact character of her enterprises. A few years ago she had entrusted me with a large envelope containing savings pass books issued by three or four different banks. At various times during the year she summoned me and the books, did God knows what kind of business and a few days later returned the envelope to me. It's Aubrey's mystery and Aubrey's business. I've never pried, I only oblige her. Not being much of a Monk fan—Luther Vandross was more her taste—she had no idea how big a favor she was asking of me on this particular day.

I dug up the envelope and set it on the kitchen table alongside the rooster drawing.

They were playing a set of Monk's thinking cap pieces. But my brain somehow wasn't turning over. What the hell did Rhode Island Red mean? And why had Wild Bill run away from me as if he'd seen Satan on my shoulder?

On second thought, though, why shouldn't he be frightened? It appeared that Inge's murderer had shouted those words before he killed her.

With great reluctance, I turned the radio off. Then I thought better of it and turned it on again, so that the sounds would continue to fill my house even if I wasn't at home.

I also took the ghoulish sketch and scotch-taped it to the refrigerator door. I stepped back and pointed threateningly at it. "Stay right there, asshole."

I stood across the street from the Emporium, just staring at the entrance. I really disliked going in there, even in the middle of the day. I didn't want to see the horny businessmen and the grinding girls or smell the stale beer and despair.

But I made myself cross over. Then, just before I reached the door, I heard a cheerful "Nan!" ring out. I turned. Who was calling my name?

"Nan! Nan!"

It wasn't Aubrey's voice.

A young white woman standing at the curb beside a van was waving to me, smiling. She was wearing an Antioch sweatshirt and jeans and in the crook of her arm was a big, healthy-looking rubber plant. Obviously she knew me, but I couldn't place her. It occurred to me then that she might be someone I'd gone to school with.

She called my name once again and made a broad gesture toward the plant, pointing at it and then nodding in my direction, as though it were meant for me. She hefted it once or twice and I thought she might drop it any moment.

I walked over to her, staring hard at her wide, friendly face, trying my best to remember her. She thrust the plant into my arms then, laughing.

I laughed too. "You mean this is mine?"

"No," she said, "but this is."

She was holding a small gun in the palm of one hand and she paused for a few seconds to let me look at it, as though she were a saleslady showing off a brooch. Then she curled her finger around the trigger and pressed the gun against the bottom of my jaw.

"Get in."

I have never been mugged. I never so much as received a spanking from my parents. And now I had the sudden image of my skull splintering. Tissue and bone and blood flying every which way. The phrase *at close range* came back to me from all the thousands of times I'd heard or read it. Then my mind went as numb as my legs and feet felt. The van door swung open and Lady Antioch pushed me in.

As the door closed behind us I stumbled over what

looked like a violin case. I was scared, but not so scared that the street musician connection wasn't immediately apparent.

The woman and I sat with our backs against one wall of the van. There was a man in the front seat. Middle-aged. Black raincoat. Short beard. Pitiless blue eyes, which he turned on me.

"We have some questions to ask you," he said wearily, as if that were an onerous thing.

The woman kept the barrel of the gun half an inch from my chin. We were both breathing heavily, sharing the same fear, I suspect—that she would have to use that gun.

"What questions?" I managed to shake out of my throat.

"Why is a nice colored girl like yourself hanging around with gangsters?"

I could only guess how stupid I must have looked at that moment, scared to death, confounded, yet half convinced that someone was playing a practical joke on me.

"What gangsters?"

"Henry Valokus."

Oh, okay. So it was a joke.

"That's ridiculous."

"He's a made member of one of the New England crime families."

Having a gun pointed at my larynx had been shock enough for one afternoon, thank you. But now I'd been given this new bit of information, casually spoken by a pale-eyed killer in a raincoat. His words had the absolute ring of veracity and so I quickly set about trying to refute them.

My knees were knocking but I had to speak up. "The

worst thing Henry's ever done is put a cassette back in the wrong case."

"I'm not going to argue with you, Nanette. You want to hang with wise guys, hang with wise guys. What I care about is you shooting off your mouth about Rhode Island Red. You are not going to shoot off your mouth anymore."

For a second there—just a second—I forgot I was being held captive. I leaned forward eagerly. "You know what it is?" I asked the interrogator. "I was only trying to find out what it means."

At his nod, the young woman beside me pushed the gun into my neck. My head slammed hard against metal.

"Okay, Nanette. I'm through talking," the grand inquisitor pronounced. "I hope you're through talking too. Because if you mention Rhode Island Red again, your big mouth won't be the only hole you've got in your head. Understand?"

I said nothing for a minute, hypnotized by those eyes.

"Do you understand me?"

I thought I'd better not force him to ask again. I nodded my understanding, the gun like dry ice on the side of my face.

The van door scraped open then. And they threw my ass out on the street like a bundle of newspapers. I landed on all fours, lathered in sweat, shaking.

I brushed myself off a little and stumbled into the Emporium. I was told by the manager, as if I were the biggest fool who ever lived, that Aubrey "doesn't work days." The bartender on duty was not named Earl and nothing I said could convince him otherwise. Furthermore, he wouldn't have called me on a bet, he said.

You've been all kinds of set-up, I thought. Better have a bourbon. The fellas who had come in for a midday fix of flaccid titties and domestic beer were casting strange looks at me. Fuck em.

All right. So two crazies had put a gun against my head and warned me about Rhode Island Red. And it had to have been Wild Bill who told them about me.

I ordered another Jack D.

All right. So I was not wrong about the words the killer had shouted in Inge's apartment.

I drank another.

All right. Henry was in the mafia.

Preposterous.

Did I drink that next one, or was it drinking me?

Two girls with bad permanents were writhing in unison. The weirdest sister act you can imagine. The men pressed closer to the stage. I needed to get out of there.

Out on Sixth Avenue, I placed one foot in front of the other. That was about the limit of my capability for the moment. I was going to walk to Henry's house, sobering up on the way. I'd straighten this shit out. Henry and I were lovers. We were friends. The only secrets involved belonged to Charlie Parker. And I was supposed to reveal those to him.

The doorman waved me in with a tip of his cap.

When Henry didn't respond to my knocks, I used my key.

The living room was empty, abandoned. Everything was gone—the Bird museum, the books, the stereo set-up. Same story in the bedroom; no clothing, no papers, no personal items—all gone. Some mischievous little fairies had blown through the apartment and left nothing but a few dust mice and the odd issue of *Stereo Review*.

I walked into the kitchen and drank water from the tap. Drank and drank and drank. And then bathed my face a little.

I stood for a long time in the center of the living room, looking from corner to corner, not an idea in hell what to do.

Where was he? Oh, Jesus, where was Henry? Kidnapped? On the lam? Dead?

I might have lost it altogether then, might have fainted dead away, or started shrieking or pounding my head against the wall. Except I had suddenly become aware of a queer odor in the room. I knew what it was and yet I didn't know.

Oh, yes, I did know. Something was burning!

In a furor I ran to all the closets and began ripping them open. Nothing was alight inside them. But in a minute I was able to trace the source of the smell.

It was in the stripped bathroom that the odor was the most intense. Still, there was no smoke. Then I understood: that odor was the aftermath of a fire. But what could have been burning? He hadn't left so much as a bar of soap in there.

I looked behind me then, at the plain white bathtub where Henry and I had showered together, come together, where he had washed and soothed me so tenderly. Fear shot through me, freezing my brain. Oh no . . . no . . . please no . . .

Slowly I pulled back the shower curtain, trying to prepare myself for the horror that was surely there waiting.

But the only thing I saw in the tub was a large scrub

bucket. I peered into it. Inside were some shreds of partially burned paper. And when I looked down at the floor I could see a trail of soot going over the lip of the tub, across the tile, and up the front of the toilet bowl.

Clearly Henry had burned a pile of papers in the pail and then flushed some of the debris down the toilet. He had vacated the premises in such a hurry that there had been no time to do the job thoroughly or clean up after himself.

I opened the linen cabinet and found a bath towel he had left behind. I took it into the living room and spread it out on the rug. Then I retrieved the pail from the tub and placed it next to the towel.

I set about reconstructing the shards of blackened paper, trying to force them, will them, back into a coherent whole. For more than an hour I worked in deadly, fevered seriousness—as though I had the tatters of Kunta Kinte's birth certificate in my fingers.

The tatters beat me, though. I couldn't make them anything close to coherent. All I had were pieces of charred paper on which hundreds of numbers in small print and the words Arrivals and Departures kept showing up. I couldn't make out much of anything else.

I stood up in disgust, legs and back aching. There were tears of frustration and hurt threatening to burst from my system and wash the room away.

And at the very moment when I lifted my boot heel to grind the papers into the towel in a fit of hatred and rage, another set of disembodied figures and letters flitted across my brain. They had to do with Inge.

As she had lain sleeping in her apartment, right after I told her Sig was dead, I had rifled through the collection of books on her shelf. In one of the steamship books, I had seen a reproduction of an art deco menu from the dining room on a luxury liner, and on the opposite page there was a reproduced Arrivals/Departures schedule.

A link between Inge—or more likely, Siggy—and Henry. What the hell was up with that? If it was a link at all. More likely, I was just grasping at straws.

Another thought occurred to me. One not nearly so fantastical. At least it had a nodding acquaintance with logic and reality: Henry wasn't interested in the same arcane kind of reading as Sig; romantic devil that he was, he was simply leaving the country—by ship.

I knelt once more and again rooted methodically through the charred pieces. I began to turn some of the larger pieces over to reveal their flip sides. There was printing on a few of the scraps, but nothing new appeared, just the same tiresome numbers and symbols. I had almost given up when one of them startled the hell out of me. "ORK HERALD TRIBU" the tiny type read, and the paper appeared to be photocopy stock. The old *New York Herald Tribune*?

Not the International Trib, which I'd read once in a while when I was in France, but the *New York Herald Tribune*. In reduced type. And Xeroxed.

Either Henry was linked to Sig by an interest in ships— which meant nothing and was hardly a crime—or he had planned an escape based on information in a newspaper that had last appeared on the stands some thirty-five years ago—which meant he was nutty as a fruit cake.

I took aim and kicked the pail halfway into the next dimension.

Back in the lobby, "Where did Mr. Valokus go?" I asked the doorman.

"Who?"

"Mr. Valokus. In 31G. He moved in a hurry, didn't he?"

"I don't believe we have a tenant by that name."

"Don't give me that shit."

"As a matter of fact, miss, I think 31G is unoccupied." His expression was serene and vacuous.

"Yes," I said at last, "you got that one right."

CHAPTER NINE

Blue Monk

Why hadn't I been more shocked when the door opened onto Henry's vacant apartment?

Because I knew—somewhere inside me—I knew. The great lover with melting eyes who was too good to be true. The Bird-struck musical naif who lived only for my black womanly wisdom. Who boiled milk for my coffee. Massaged my feet. The lonely Greek émigré, who had, he said, like me, bummed around Europe. Who late at night reminisced with me about the cakes in this patisserie in Montmartre and the blood sausages at the brasserie next to the jazz joint on the rue de Buci. Kind, sensitive, generous. My Henry. Whose mouth I dreamed about. The mafia lackey. Ha ha. Gotcha, Nan. You dumb bitch.

Too bad for him, his scam got blown before he got what he wanted from me. Too bad for me, I'd never really know what that was.

Was Henry dead or alive now? Had those creeps in the van gotten to him? Was he a real criminal whose scene with me was part of a mob plan? Or was the thing with me for real and somehow interfering with what he was supposed to be accomplishing for the mob? Either way, I guess he had fucked up. And he must have been pretty scared to pull up stakes that quickly.

Scared. Like that old bastard, Wild Bill. Who had clearly put those people in the van onto me. I wished I had him in my hands at that moment. I could have shown him a couple of things about playing the blues. And I'd have begun by shoving that fucking harmonica up where the sun never shines.

Mom called. I know because I listened to her leave me a message.

Aubrey called to find out what I had wanted yesterday at the Emporium.

My prospective music coach called to invite me to a party on the Upper West Side, a party for Monk.

Walter called to say what's happening? His voice faltered then and he hung up.

I drank vats of camomile tea. And when that didn't work I found and played the Carmen McRae album that she had autographed for my pop back in 1959. And when that didn't work I made a rogue's gallery of the faces of all the tenor players whose records I had been collecting for the past ten years. And when that didn't work I paced.

The knocking at the front door was loud and desperate. I stood in the middle of the room as the pounding continued. What would I do if it was Henry? I realized how much I wanted it to be him. How much I wanted him to walk in here and laugh at me for thinking my weird nightmares were reality. To tell me I'd been asleep for two days—dreamed all of it—and he was here to wake me with some sprightly Beaujolais and hundreds of kisses on my eyelids.

It wasn't Henry Valokus I saw through the peephole. It was Walter. And he was holding a bunch of flowers.

When I let him in, I could see that the flowers were only part of the deal. He had brought take-out fried chicken and sweet potato pie from a place we used to frequent, up on Amsterdam. He had also brought a couple of arcane Irish beers. Finally, he was toting a huge cardboard box that carried the Hugo Boss label; he had obviously bought a new suit.

I suppose Walter could see how crazy and depressed I was, but he never said a word about it. He just set the table quietly, and when the meal was over, he asked, equally quietly, whether "my thing was over now."

"Yeah, it's over," I confirmed.

I did the dishes while he searched the TV guide, looking, I knew, for exhibition basketball games. For the past year and a half he'd been paying for cable service, which was kind of a waste given my crummy black and white set, but there was no way he was going to miss a single Knicks game. I watched him fiddle with the channels, his sleeves rolled up.

Mom liked Walter, she always had. I guess he looked like a real provider, and she figured, correctly, that I was going to require a fair amount of being provided for. I glanced over at him from time to time while I cleaned up in the kitchen. I didn't know how to begin to tell him about all the things that had happened to me in the past few weeks. Especially about Henry. So I put it all away for the night.

I set a bowl of popcorn in front of him, the kind with fake red pepper sprinkled on it, his favorite. He looked up briefly and laid an appreciative hand on my butt for a minute before turning back to the game.

"I'm whipped, Walter," I said. "Going to bed."

"I work all day but you're whipped. Nobody like you, Nan."

I sat up in bed thinking about the dark green sheets on Henry's bed, about the frantic swiftness of Wild Bill's gait, about the feel of that gun on my skin, and about a terrified young Dominican enunciating the goofy words of a country and western song.

What had I really done to Diego's words?

Had I massaged them into the phrase Rhode Island Red? Or translated them? Or debauched them? I had put the phrase together. Diego had not.

But I was a translator. I knew that words lie.

After all, take Verlaine.

> *Je suis un berceau*
> *Qu'une main balance*
> *Au creux d'un caveau . . .*

Some have said this means:

> *I am a cradle being rocked*
> *by a hand in the*
> *center of a crypt . . .*

But someone else maintains it means:

> *Deep in the hollow earth*
> *my childhood is ravaged by*
> *a fist . . .*

Ask Verlaine which is closer to the truth.

But Verlaine is long dead.

Diego, however, wasn't. Maybe if he were presented with those very words, they'd mean something to him.

They had meant something to Charlie Conlin and to Inge. I was fairly certain the two of them had died because of those words.

I heard a muffled cheer from the next room. Somebody must have made a basket or something.

It was only a little after noon, but the day was over for the bulk of the workers in the flower district. Their shift began at three or four in the morning. I looked up and down the cramped streets with their double rows of potted plants squeezing the pedestrians into single file, and I wondered where the workers ate their lunch at, say, 6:30 A.M. What would you have for lunch at six-thirty in the morning? There had been this guy, Dale, a fellow grad school student, who liked prowling the streets at all hours of the morning. He used to take me into these funky coffee shops—places where the transsexuals were the respectable folks and the rest of the patrons went down the social ladder from there—where he would down gallons of shitty coffee and natter at me in that sincere Marxist way of his about the hidden injuries of race and class. I sometimes thought he got off on people assuming I was a hooker.

What made me think of that? I was wasting time. I was stalling, postponing my entrance into the wholesale market where Diego worked. But I picked up my feet and walked toward the place.

I evoked a couple of half-hearted lewd remarks from the guys lounging outside the front door. Ignoring them, I looked up at the window of the apartment where Inge had died.

An old man was slowly squeegee-ing a sheet metal table on which a million flowers had been trimmed. Wet leaves and petals clung to his trouser legs like appliqué.

"Is Diego here?" I asked him.

He gestured to the rear of the room. I walked through a set of swinging doors and into a dingy room with nine lockers nailed against one wall. In front of them was a long wooden bench where Diego sat lacing up his sneakers. Beside him was an open beer can in a paper bag and a cigarette left burning at the edge of the seat.

I called his name.

The boy looked up dumbly.

"Diego?" I called again.

It took a full thirty seconds for him to react, and when he did he only heaved a tremendous sigh. Diego was good and high.

"Do you remember me?"

He swayed a little on the bench. "Yeah. You one of the lady cops."

"No, I'm not, Diego. I came in with them, but I'm not a cop."

He smirked then, enjoying a joke I wasn't in on.

I sat down at the edge of the bench. Not only was Diego stoned, he looked as if he hadn't slept in days.

"I need to talk to you for a minute, Diego."

No answer.

"It's about Inge, the woman who was killed upstairs."

"What?" He sat a bit straighter then, and suddenly ran his hands over the postadolescent stubble on his chin.

"I want to know if Inge ever mentioned something

called Rhode Island Red to you. Do you ever remember hearing those words before—from her or anybody else?"

"Say what?"

"Rhode . . . Island . . . Red."

"No. No. I don't remember." He found his cigarette and took a desperate pull on it but it had gone out.

"Are you sure, Diego? See, maybe when you thought you heard—"

He picked up his beer then but apparently the can was empty. I guess that tore it, because in a second he was on his feet, hurling the empty can against the nearest locker.

"I didn't hear nothing, man!" he bellowed. "I don't know what those stupid fucking words are!" Next, he grabbed the bench itself, nearly knocking me to the floor, and sent that flying against the wall. His little frame was trembling with rage.

I wanted to get out of there but I was afraid any sudden move might send him after me. He took a step toward me. I tensed, searching the room for something to fend him off with.

But Diego had no more violence in him. He staggered over to the lockers and collapsed against them. "Don't you think I remember everything she said to me?" he choked out. "Don't you think I know what she said, man?" Then he was overtaken by the sobs.

Oh wow. Damn. He had been in love with her.

"Diego, will you—"

"Fuck you, man! Get out of here. Get out and leave me alone. I wish I was dead, I wish I was with her—dead. I don't care, I don't care, I don't care. I just hope that fucking cop of hers is burning in hell. I just wanna see how much she loves him now."

I took a couple of tentative steps in his direction. When he turned toward me his face was soggy, old. Then he opened his mouth and a raw, primordial scream came out. The elderly man I'd seen earlier appeared then, along with one of my admirers from out front. I pushed my way past them.

Out on the street again, I walked quickly, taking deep breaths of the heady green air. Talk about burning in hell, Diego's pain had scorched me. I wanted to put some distance between me and all that throbbing hurt.

I didn't get very far.

That fucking cop of hers. See how much she loves him now.

That cop. Diego wasn't talking about Leman Sweet. He meant Charlie Conlin—Sig. Except, Inge didn't know Sig was a cop. So how did Diego know? Unless . . . Oh.

There had been nothing in the papers about Sig's death. Presumably because the police had suppressed the story. The murder of a poor blind girl and her dog had made a splash in the news, but there had been no mention of a lover killed a few days earlier. Certainly there had been no mention of Charlie Conlin at the time Diego was questioned.

The lovesick little b-boy from the Dominican Republic seemed to know one secret too many.

I called Leman Sweet—again.

Diego had obtained a fresh beer. He was just leaving when Leman Sweet swung into the locker room, with me two paces behind him. We three had a kind of slapstick collision in the doorway.

The boy stood paralyzed, his eyes locked with the massive cop's. Sweet's big booted foot spasmed suddenly and Diego landed upright on the bench he had tried to destroy fifteen minutes ago.

Sweet strode over to the boy. "You got something to say to me, don't you, Pancho?"

Diego only winced.

Sweet snatched him up off the seat as though Diego were a shopping bag full of air. Fingers against his throat, he flung the boy in my direction.

I screamed and tried to throw my arm protectively across Diego's chest.

The detective sent me halfway across the room with a shrug of one shoulder.

"Don't kill him!" I shouted.

"Open that motherfucking locker, you," Sweet boomed.

"Open it yourself," the kid wheezed.

Sweet hit him in the stomach savagely and Diego crumpled.

I moaned then and covered my eyes.

Sweet took a fistful of the boy's hair and twisted him over to the wall. "Open it!"

"Open it!" I cried, echoing him. "He'll kill you!"

Diego complied.

"You move and I'll shoot your heart out," Sweet told him. The detective thrust both hands into the locker and began pulling objects out in a frenzy. Diego stood there maniacally squeezing his palms together. "What's the matter, you think I'm gonna break your crack pipe? What am I gonna find in here, Diego, huh? What am I gonna find?"

Sweet picked through tee-shirts and hairbrushes and jock straps and plastic shampoo containers, heedlessly flinging each thing away from him. Then he came out with what appeared to be a crowbar and a small precision drill. "Somebody started working on the cylinder of your door lock that night. Probably using just this kinda stuff," he said over his shoulder at me. He placed the objects gently on the floor.

Next came a grimy white envelope closed with a paperclip. He spilled out the contents onto the wooden bench: photographs. He looked through them quickly, replaced them, walked over to the silent Diego and slammed the envelope into his ashen face. Once Sweet had handcuffed the kid, he took the envelope and tossed it over to me.

I opened the flap and removed the stack of photos. They were all of Inge, in various stages of nudity. She may or may not have known she was being photographed—or spied on—whatever.

A hundred questions were running through my mind. About Diego and Inge. About Inge and Sig. About love turned to madness, and madness to murder. Was Diego, too, part of the Rhode Island Red mystery? Was he possibly connected to Henry? Or was his part in all this mayhem and unhappiness strictly localized, coincidental—having only to do with his obsession with the blind woman?

I looked up from the pictures at that moment, looked across the room to see Leman Sweet aiming his revolver at the bridge of Diego's nose. I just stood there waiting for the roar of the gun. No matter how horrible it was going to be, I knew I wouldn't be able to look away.

"You killed my partner, didn't you, scum? You put that ice pick in Charlie."

Diego looked right into the barrel of that gun. Slowly, slowly, he raised his hands, almost in a gesture of supplication and began to nod his head.

Just like in the movies, the action seemed to take place through a curtain of gauze, slow, so slow, everything happening in slow motion. Sweet pulling back the hammer of the gun. Diego importuning, nodding. Me doing my imitation of Buckwheat.

Then I heard Sweet reciting the Miranda warnings about the right to silence and hiring an attorney. He was reholstering his gun.

"I've got to ask you some questions," I said to him when he had finished.

"Uh uh. You ain't got to ask me nothing. Only question now is whether we nail him for one murder or two."

CHAPTER TEN

Epistrophy

 I wasn't expecting the NYPD to give me a medal for finding the murderer of an undercover cop. And they didn't disappoint. I got zip.

Madder fack, as I'd once heard a TV evangelist say, they appeared to be pissed at me for showing that Sig's death had nothing to do with the investigation he and Leman were part of. The killing of poor Sig/Charlie was motivated by nothing more conspiratorial than unrequited love . . . jealousy. Diego's formal confession had stated that he never knew Sig was a cop until the night he killed him, when he'd discovered Sig's ID taped to his leg holster.

As for the world's nastiest civil servant, Detective Leman Sweet, he seemed even more eager to get shed of me than I was him. After Diego was behind bars—his room on Rivington Street swept clean of all the sicko bondage magazines and his pitifully inchoate love letters to Inge—I had tried to talk to Sweet about the crazed chain of events that had linked us all. But he was resolutely not interested. The days went by. And the autumn weather turned the leaves to flame. There were no more mystery calls summoning me up blind alleys. No white girls shoving pistols up my nose. And, to be sure, no Henry Valokus.

He and whoever it was he was working with, working for, or running from, had obviously determined I wasn't a player in their game. For which I had only to be grateful. And so I tried to bury the Rhode Island Red business as deep as the dead leaves of those first yellow roses.

If only I played the sax half as well as I played the fool. Ah, I could only try. Jefferson, my coach, said I was making progress even if I didn't know it yet. I kept to the street gig, though, and that along with the few bucks coming in from the translation work I did for an avant garde French publishing house kept me afloat.

Not to mention the help I got from Walt. He never knew what a beacon in the darkness he was for me. Oh, our carnal thing was still in place, but that wasn't the main thing for me anymore. After all this time, I found out I could sort of talk to Walter about things—sort of. He tried to listen a little when I talked about Verlaine and I tried to listen when he worried aloud about the coming merger at work or bitched about the snotty fag at the tie counter at Barney's.

I needed a substitute ear these days because, as of late, Aubrey was powerfully distracted. By something I couldn't blame her for: my girl was in love.

I'd never seen Aubrey goofy before. Up until then, I thought her constitutionally incapable of it. But there she was—acting goofy. It was fifty percent treat and fifty percent pain in the ass. But she had my patience and indulgence coming to her, given all the dumb crushes and mad *affaires de coeur* she'd nursed me through over the years.

Her man was named Jeremy. He was tall, slender, fall down dead gorgeous, black as night—*and British*! And every time he dropped a consonant or called her "luv," she just about came in her jumpsuit.

Jeremy was actually more suitable for me. Yeah, I know how trifling that makes me sound. All I mean is, in a parallel universe, he and I probably would have got down immediately, as if preordained to do so. Jeremy was a working class genius who went to Oxford and now made his living as a music critic—everything from Schoenberg to Hendrix. But his passion was jazz. He was quick and hip and worldly and traveled and charming. He had taken time off from his music magazine job to write a book on Fletcher Henderson and was in New York relaxing after having turned a first draft over to his editor.

Lucky for the lovers, we were in *this* universe, where Jeremy had walked into the Emporium one night in the company of a friend of his (a drag queen who calls herself Velveeta) and had taken one look at Aubrey and . . . Well, it makes me rethink who was predestined to be with who. Lord, were they hot together, Aubrey and Jeremy. And it was out there for everybody to see. I was truly happy for her.

One of Jeremy's paychecks which had been waylaid for weeks finally arrived. He wanted to celebrate. So he invited Walt and me to join him and Aubrey at a posh supper club uptown where a pianist he knew was performing.

Didn't exactly sound like my scene, a stodgy, rip-off

East Side *boîte*. An ungracious Walter put it best, perhaps: the grub's gonna stink and we gonna be the stone only niggers in the place.

It didn't help matters that he and Aubrey did not get along. But I went to work on him; and when the appointed evening rolled around, after he had diddled me nicely in the shower and fought me for a place in front of my full-length mirror, Walt was brushing off his latest finery and pestering me to finish my make-up. We were only ten minutes late arriving.

Aubrey had never been a heavy drinker. But she was doing margaritas that night, just to keep pace with Jeremy, who had an apparent fondness for hundred-proof Absolut. "Vodka, Nan?" he offered when Walter and I slid into their booth. Only he pronounced it "vodker."

"Why not, old bean?" I accepted.

I had spent time with Jeremy on two occasions before that night. He and Walter, however, had never met. First off, Walter was floored by the accent. It was almost as if he didn't believe that was Jeremy's real voice. No real black man could sound like that, he seemed to believe. But as we all drank and began to relax, the two men seemed to be stumbling their way onto common ground. It was only when Walt started talking basketball that he lost Jeremy, who sat through Walt's breathless recitations of Patrick Ewing's stats in dead silence.

"Never went in much for sports," Jeremy said finally. "I was a wash at football. Don't mind skiing once in a while though."

Walter looked at me in a kind of horror, then at Aubrey, and finally back at Jeremy, who, Walt had plainly decided, was a Martian.

In the quietly tasteful, tastefully quiet room, Aubrey erupted with raucous laughter. Then she turned to her beloved and kissed him on the mouth. "You know, Jeremy, Nan's a writer too," she said when that was finished. "They published something she wrote about Remy."

"Remy? Who's that, luv?"

"Rimbaud," I explained. "It was in the world's littlest little magazine."

"Smashing. I've got a soft spot for the surrealists myself. Mate of mine wrote a book about Robert Desnos, you know—the poet who survived Buchenwald."

I thought I heard Walter groan just then. But he needn't have worried. What promised to be a highly effete conversation was cut short when Jeremy's friend, pianist Brad Weston, took his seat.

The trio led by Weston was good, damn good. I could tell by the crisp solemnity of the chords introducing "Maiden Voyage" that they would be. There followed a heartbreaking version of "I'll Be Seeing You." And Weston's solo on "My Foolish Heart" quite literally made me cry. If his mission was to bum out this crowd, he was succeeding brilliantly.

When the set was over and the applause had abated, the pianist headed over to our table.

"Trriffick set, mate—trrifick!" Jeremy said, standing to greet him. "Wife didn't leave you or anything, did she?"

Weston smiled a little and shook his head.

Jeremy made the introductions and Walt, Aubrey, and I supplied the compliments. After a few moments of small talk with us, the pianist pushed his scotch aside and removed his eyeglasses in order to massage his temple.

"Headache?" Jeremy asked him.

He shook his head. "No, no, man. I'm just tired. I went to a funeral today and it just wasted me. It was so . . . terrible . . . so sad and terrible."

"Who died?"

"Old cat. He was a trumpeter. Died of a stroke. They collected money at the union hall to bury him. Name was Heywood Tuttle. Ever hear of him?"

Jeremy shook his head. "I can't place him. The name rings some kind of bell though, however faint."

"Faint is about right, man. Couldn't have been more than ten people at the cat's funeral. It's like he fell through a hole in life, you know. Good musician. Played most of his life up in Providence. I think he gigged once or twice with Bird, as a matter of fact. But he was on junk a lot of the time. Got busted a lot and spent years in the joint.

"By the time he got to New York he was too old to be a junkie. He was just another wino, I guess. Pitiful. I saw him once in a while around Times Square. He was begging for quarters. Playing a damn harmonica and looking like something from the circus. God, I hated seeing him like that. I gave him ten bucks.

"The guy that collected the bread for the funeral told me Tuttle had been flopping at a tenement over by the entrance to the Lincoln Tunnel. An old man like that stuck in all those fumes. Sick. Choking. Forgotten. Like he never gave a thing to the world. Can you imagine that?"

Yes, I could.

If nobody else could, I could.

He was talking about Wild Bill! Oh Jesus.

So Wild Bill—or Heywood Tuttle—was from Provi-

dence. From Rhode Island! New England. Like Henry Valokus and that "family" he was said to be part of.

So Wild Bill had some connection, however fleeting, to
Charlie Parker. Charlie Parker was Henry's *raison d'être,*
or so he had claimed.

So Rhode Island Red wasn't a thing but a person. Tuttle
himself was Rhode Island Red—right? But how was it
possible that burned out, bad-tempered little Wild Bill had
been the cause of all the death and mayhem?

And then, what had the kidnapping episode been about?
Why did those idiots go to such lengths to get me to stop
talking about Rhode Island Red? And why hadn't they
killed me if shutting me up was so important?

And what did any of it have to do with Henry Valokus?

I couldn't answer a single one of those questions—yet.

This had all the elements of a film student's low-budget
homage to Godard—a saintly blind girl; a carful of killers;
a brutal policeman and a cast of doppelgängers. Everybody
had been leading a double life. There were two Sigs, two
Wild Bills, two Henrys. I had tried to get them all out of
my mind and my heart, but they just would not stay dead
for me. Back they came, like a song.

The waste of the whole situation was devastating. Wild
Bill, once a good musician, his vitality drained, lost to junk
or juice, along with his talent and his pride. Siggy, barely
thirty years old, murdered horribly. Diego, friendless and
little more than a boy, who'd likely spend the remainder of
his life in prison. Henry, who might or might not actually
be dead but who was just as lost to me one way as the
other.

I must have turned sickly green. Because Aubrey and Jeremy, Brad Weston and Walter were all looking at me with

fear and concern. I tried to tell them I was okay, but they hustled me out of there and into a taxi.

No, I couldn't help thinking about the waste. And I couldn't help thinking I had to be the one to put a stop to it. But first I had to understand it.

CHAPTER ELEVEN

Straight, No Chaser

 I recall vividly the first time I was allowed to study in the magnificent main Manhattan library all on my own. I was eleven years old, too cool to go over and pet the lions, but wildly in love with them, secretly. Daddy had dropped me off that morning—school was on spring hiatus—with lunch money and threats to my life if I dared leave the reading room and go traipsing unaccompanied across Forty-second Street. I was doing big time research for my paper on Japanese poetry, thinking of making a living as a haiku poet.

The library had fallen into awful disrepair in my life-time, the grime and neglect all but burying its majesty. But a major renovation effort over the past three years or so has restored its grandeur. And now, not only does the facade gleam and the lions stand proudly, the park behind it is splendidly kept as well; not one but two lovely cafés have opened—one on either side of the stairs leading up to the entrance; and high atop the building there is a grand style restaurant, with prices to match, from which you can look down into the stacks of the circulating library! A bit much, maybe. But on the whole I approve.

I could have gone to NYU, or borrowed a card from a friend with library privileges up at Columbia. But I figured the public library to be a much better bet for the kind of research I needed to do—nothing arcane, like images of water in the poems of Basho. No. More like pop culture.

"V" as in "Valokus." There was nothing so difficult about that. I was trying to treat the Henry Valokus mystery like a paper I had absolutely no heart for but knew I'd have to tackle before the semester was over.

Who was it who first glamorized the image of the mobster? Was it old Hollywood? Was it Al Capone? Scott Fitzgerald with Gatsby's bootlegging? The mob in all its sundry manifestations seems to be the source of ongoing, inexhaustible fascination. More books get published about gangsters than about women in rotten marriages, which is saying something.

Just what made us so interested in criminals, anyway? Personally, I blamed Coppola for making Al Pacino and Robert De Niro look so edible in the *Godfather* movies. I must have been about twelve years old when I saw those films on television and I sure wanted me an Italian. Of course the sad realization that blacks and Italians in American cities are locked in a filthy embrace of loathing and violence against one another for as long as the two races exist was still ahead of me then. Still, while I wouldn't drive through parts of Bensonhurst on a bet, I've never met an Italian from Italy that I didn't get along with.

I started with the old newspapers and magazines.

There were mafia bigwig profiles, mob family genealogies, Cosa Nostra wars, inter-ethnic mob contacts, favorite mafia recipes, gangster angst, coming of age horror stories, interior decorating tips.

I skimmed them all.

Didn't see Valokus. But there was Vincent . . . Little Vince . . . Big Vince . . . Vinnie the Bull . . . Vick the Gimp. Val the Hulk. Vicious Vittorio. Vaseline Eddie.

There was Henry the Barber, Henry the Bomber, Sweet Henry, Hungry Henry, Henry the Hangman.

But those preposterous monikers that shared Henry's initials were about as close as I came to locating Henry Valokus.

Pop out of there, Henry, I whispered to each fresh roll of microfilm. But Henry didn't pop. He wasn't in the newspapers. He wasn't in the magazines. He was no pop idol at all.

Then, undaunted, I gathered to my table virtually all the current titles on the Mob, or La Cosa Nostra, or the Mafia, or the Syndicate. There were fat books by scholars and memoirs by reputed members of the organization, serious sociological treatments of the subject which deplored the stereotypes, bad screenplays, good screenplays, transcripts of crime commission hearings. There were novels that spoofed the mob, recasting its members as comic figures and grisly photo books that gave the lie to the laughter. There was a bonanza right in front of me.

"V" for Valokus.

Eighteen books later I hadn't found a single reference to him.

Now what was I supposed to do? Knock on the door of

one of those downtown social clubs and ask if they had any graduation yearbooks?

Wearily, I started returning all the books. I believed those crazies in the van. I believed the gun against my head. If Henry really was a mobster—why hadn't he popped out?

Either because Henry Valokus was not his real name or because he was just too lowly a soldier.

It had been a while since I'd spent the day on a hard wooden chair in the library. My back hurt and I was hungry. I'd had it for the day. I trudged down the marble stairs of the main entrance and toward the exit. But I didn't leave. I had had a perfectly brilliant idea. Twenty-five cents worth.

I rushed to the phone and dialed Aubrey.

I'd remembered her talking about a man—Aubrey had told me about him not long after she started dancing at the Emporium. He dropped in a few times a week to collect the receipts from the safe. He signed the checks, hired and fired. He knew every single person who worked in the club. He was the man.

"Who is it?"

I could hear the tiredness in her voice. I knew that once again I had awakened her.

"It's me, Aubrey," I said apologetically. "I'm really sorry. But it's kind of an emergency."

I heard mumbling in the distance.

"Guess I woke Jeremy up too."

"Morning, Nan," he called into the receiver.

"Jeremy says you got more emergencies than anybody he knows."

"Really? Well, tell him when his little book gets published I'll treat it as a matter of no urgency whatever."

"Ima let you tell him that yourself, Nan. What's the matter now?"

"Can you get me an appointment with that gangster who manages the Emporium?"

"You mean Justin Thom?"

"Yes. He's a gangster, isn't he?"

"Who ain't?"

"When do you think you might see him again?"

"I don't know—maybe tonight. Nan, what the hell you want with crazy Justin?"

"It's too long a story," I said in exasperation. "Look, I know he likes you. Do you think you could get him to talk to me? Tell him I swear I won't take up too much of his time."

"You shoulda gone to Paris, Nan."

"I know. I want to let you get back to sleep now. Please, just call him for me. Tell him I don't want to know anything about his business and tell him it won't take long."

She didn't answer for the longest time. I could hear her lighting a cigarette and inhaling.

Then she said: "Okay. Call me back in twenty minutes."

I hung up and rummaged through the postcards section of the library bookstore. I bought one: an old William Claxton photo, a beautiful night-time shot of a bass player shielding his ax from the rain.

When I called Aubrey back the line was busy. I went back to the bookstore and bought another card; this one of a young Langston Hughes uptown.

I called again five minutes later.

Justin Thom would see me about 1 P.M. in his office on West Eighteenth Street, a place called Tower Printing.

"I guess next time I see you you'll tell me what the fuck you doing, Nan."

"Trust me," I replied. "Happy dreams, you two."

About five minutes to one I took the elevator up to the fifth floor of the dingy building which housed Tower Printing.

I rang a buzzer outside the peeling door. An answering buzz let me in.

There was no printing equipment that I could see on the premises. There were no computers, no typewriters, no files. There was only one desk and one chair in the waiting room. The walls were bare. The floor was highly polished.

A stout, black, middle-aged woman wearing a gaily colored head wrap sat behind the desk. She was cussing bitterly as she fiddled with a boom box.

I greeted her. "Good afternoon. I have an appointment with—"

"Through there," she said, cutting me off. Then she added: "Don't knock. He doesn't like people to knock."

Justin Thom looked up when I entered the room. He was seated on a rattan sofa with purple cushions, reading the *Village Voice*. There was no desk in the room, only the sofa and two matching armchairs.

"Mister Thom?" I asked, taken aback and, I feared, unable to mask my astonishment.

First of all, his faded designer jeans and tight-fitting studded leather jacket—he wore no shirt underneath and he was working on a little belly—made him look like some suburban closet case on Christopher Street twenty years ago. Yes, he was as gay as ticks are tiny.

That seemed pretty original for the mob. Or were they a good deal more enlightened than I was giving them credit for? Then again, maybe I was the one who was behind the times. Perhaps tolerance—shall we say, affirmative action—had reached even into the cradle of crime.

Justin's hair was coiffed almost unto death—long, peroxided, tied at the back with a velvet band.

And, perhaps most startling of all, he was no older than I.

"Aubrey's friend?" he asked.

"Yes. Thank you for seeing me."

He looked me over, brazenly, critically, before offering me a seat. There was a hint of distaste in his gaze, and more than a little confusion.

It was apparent that I had discomfited him. And then suddenly I realized why. I realized what he was thinking.

"No, no," I said reassuringly, "I don't want to dance in your club. I'm not here for that. I'm not looking for *any* kind of job, as a matter of fact."

His face relaxed somewhat.

I jumped right in. "I need information," I said.

"What kind of information?"

"About the mob."

He grinned. "Is that right?"

"Yes. I need some information about someone who's in the mob. Or at least I think he is. That's why I'm here."

He burst into hearty laughter. "That's a good one, child. I never knew Aubrey to be a practical joker."

"She isn't. I'm serious."

He hesitated for a moment, fear creeping around the edges of his expression. "You wearing a wire or something equally ridiculous?"

"No, I'm not."

"Reporter?"

"Not smart enough for that."

"That's very funny too. Now tell me why you picked me to give you a mafia lesson."

"Aubrey says everyone in her business is either in the mob or owned by the mob. To hear her tell it, it's an occupational hazard."

"Let me tell you something, girlfriend. Listen to *anything* Aubrey's got to say. She's rarely wrong about anything." He batted his eyelids playfully. "So, okay I'm a mob-stah. But to tell you the truth, I'm really a bartender. From Lockport, Indiana. White bread as they come. That is, I *used* to be a bartender. Until I was . . . discovered . . . at the soda fountain."

"By way of the West Street bars?"

"You're not that dumb, miss."

"My name is Nanette."

"Nice name for a stripper." He fired up a Benson & Hedges 100 with a day-glo colored disposable lighter.

Justin didn't have to offer me a cigarette twice. I pounced as soon as he turned the pack my way. I hadn't had a cigarette like that in so long.

"Mr. Thom, I'll come to the point. I'm hoping you know a . . . crook . . . whose name is Henry Valokus. I seem to be in a fair amount of trouble and so is he, I think. He may not know it but he needs my help. I'm . . . in love with Henry Valokus . . . and I can't find him. Can you help?"

"You're in love," he said slowly, "with who?"

"Henry Valokus. Valokus. Comma. Henry. Do you know him?"

"What did he do—knock you up?"

"Nothing like that."

He blew smoke at the ceiling and repeated dully, "You're in love—with Henry Valokus."

"That's what I said, Bub."

After his coughing fit was all played out, he rose from the sofa and came to stand very close to my chair.

"But he's an asshole, isn't he?"

"Excuse me, Mr. Thom, but could you please just get to the point?"

"If he's the same guy I'm thinking of, he's a bit of a boob. Kind of looks like Napoleon, dresses like Victor Mature?"

"Dresses like who?"

"Never mind. Comes out of Providence, right? Talks with an accent."

"That's him."

"If I tell you what I know about him, will you promise not to die of boredom?"

"Promise."

Justin Thom stretched, walked back to the sofa, sat down, crossed his legs and lit another cigarette.

"It's a ten-second story, really. He was born over in Europe but he grew up in Rhode Island, which means he worked for the Calvalcante family, out of Boston. They run the rackets in Hartford, Providence, New Haven.

"Valokus was busted for—oh, shit, what was it?—right—a hijacking charge. He ratted out somebody or other. Not a big muckety muck, really, but still, the Feds put him in Witness Protection. But when the case came to court Valokus got shredded by the defense attorneys. Prosecution's case fell all to shit. Case dismissed."

"Then what happened?"

"They kicked his ass out of the Protection Program. Cut him loose. They're some vengeful mothers, you know."

"Then what?"

"He did time on the original hijacking charge."

"And when he was released?"

"Don't tell me that schmuck is good in bed."

"Listen, mister . . ."

"Okay, Okay." He shook his head. "Jeez. Straight people," he said in puzzlement. "Oh, well, judge not lest ye be judged, as the good book tells us. I mean, Miss Susan Hayward wasn't the greatest actress who ever drew breath but I'm ready to kick ass if anybody says a word against her."

"Please, what happened to Henry Valokus after he got out of prison?"

"Nothing happened, far as I know. Nothing at all. Don't you get it?"

"No."

"Any other rat would have been gotten to. Either in jail or out of jail. Someone would have whacked him long ago. He'd be dead and buried. But Valokus was such a pitiful rat . . . such a buffoon . . . that even if there was a contract out on him, there weren't any takers. The studio didn't pick up his option."

"Poor Henry," I said.

Justin laughed and coughed and laughed and coughed. "Now you take me. If I ratted out one of my associates, you'd probably find me in a Hefty bag on Christopher Street. Half of me, that is. You'd still be looking for the other half. And I'm just a poor little faggot they promoted from the ranks. Valokus could have been a *real* bad guy."

"So I guess you wouldn't have any idea where I might find him—where he might be hiding out?"

He laughed again. "You mean like the Gangster Arms on West Fourteenth Street? No, sugar, not a clue."

I thanked him and rose to leave.

"Wait just a sec," he called.

I turned back and met his eyes.

"Listen, Nanny. I don't know whether I buy your story or not. You don't look like the kind of girl who'd be fucking a guy like Valokus, no matter what they say about Greeks. Anyhoo, I guess I've always been a sucker for a smash-up in love."

"A what?"

"A smash-up. I call all women 'smash-ups.' At any rate, I told you what I know because you're Aubrey's friend. And Aubrey is real good for my business. I owe her. I don't even think I have to remind you to be cool, but I will anyway. You know what I'm saying?"

Actually, I hadn't a clue what he was saying. But I nodded—gravely, sagely—and moved out of the door.

I turned into the first coffee shop I saw. The ubiquitous Greek coffee shop. I ordered coffee and one of those lard-laden muffins and I sat at the counter thinking dark thoughts.

Those unfriendly white folks in the van had not lied. Dear Henry Valokus was a criminal. But, according to Justin Thom, not a very successful one. A schmuck, he'd called Henry. A buffoon. Well, Henry wasn't the first man I had found endearingly eccentric, while the world judged him a great deal more harshly. But a boob? An asshole? I stared down at the countertop, hurt, ashamed somehow, as if someone were calling me those names. Like the kids bad-mouthing Aubrey, my best friend.

So my lost love really was from Providence. Just like Wild Bill, aka Heywood Tuttle. Both show up in New York. Both connected to street musicians—Valokus to me, Wild Bill to the murdered blind girl. Providence. Some divine Providence. How many miles from Providence to Provence?

At least he hadn't lied about being Greek.

This poem was beginning to unravel. Both from Providence. One actually played with Bird. One claimed to be obsessed with Bird.

Where had their connection started? Was Wild Bill the gardener for the Valokus estate? Not bloody likely. Did he sell moonshine to Henry's father? Where did the thread begin and where did it end?

Well, wait a minute. I already knew where it ended, didn't I? Brad Weston, the melancholy pianist, had told us that poor Heywood Tuttle had lived his last days in a squalid tenement that hovered over the entrance to the Lincoln Tunnel.

I walked west to the Tunnel and hopscotched through the traffic. Motorists flinched when they saw me, thinking I was one of those mad window wipers.

Up loomed a single half block of tenements, an island in the center of a traffic mess. Half of the island was filled with crumbling condemned houses, many of them boarded up. The sidewalk had been all but removed.

But four buildings remained. All occupied. I wondered how the residents negotiated back and forth late at night.

The fumes and honking noise were almost overwhelming. It was hell. And the devil might be living behind any door.

I pressed myself against a wall and waited. Tuttle had lived in one of those buildings. But which one? And how could I get inside without someone calling the police?

The spirit was upon me, or with me. Five minutes later an old man with the rawboned look of the covered wagon pioneer menfolk walked out of one of the buildings carrying a torn carton which he dropped unceremoniously at the curbside trash collection area. Inside the box, among the debris, were the red shoes I'd seen Wild Bill wearing.

"Excuse me!" I called out hastily to the old man before he could disappear into the building again. "Excuse me, but I think you knew my grandfather."

He looked at me, not comprehending.

"Wild Bill was my grandfather."

The old man squinted at me, removed the cigar and pronounced: "Hickok?"

For a moment I didn't understand. Then I got the joke. And I laughed.

"My name's Reardon," the old man said, "and I don't know any Wild Bill."

"I mean Heywood Tuttle."

Mr. Reardon pulled on the long string and there was light in the basement. Three cats flashed by us, headed toward the far wall.

"Friends of mine," Mr. Reardon said.

Mr. Reardon was really quite nice to me. He explained that my grandfather had been a decent man at heart, it had just been "the drink" that made life so tough for him. It happened "to a lot of us," he said. He was so sorry not to have made it to the funeral, but he'd be pleased to show me the few things left in Mr. Tuttle's room at the time of his passing.

"You know, I always thought it was interesting how Heywood never talked much about his past. I knew there had to be some kin of his somewhere in the world. Isn't it just the goddamnest thing! Your grandpa dies just a week or so before you find him?"

"Yes sir it is." I sniffled once and wiped at an elephant tear.

"He was a pretty peculiar man, that's for sure. To this day I don't know where he was most of that week before he died. He'd paid his rent, but don't look like he barely ever slept at home."

"Well, you know musicians. I'm sure he had a reason."

"Another thing," Mr. Reardon added. "I always asked your grandfather why he didn't buy a bed. Said he preferred that old cot." And he nodded toward the nasty thing. " 'Course it's yours if you want it. It's only right, you being kin. But I just thought somebody else might be able to use it."

"Keep it with my blessing, Mr. Reardon."

He showed me the other pitiful things Wild Bill had possessed: a shaky bureau with the bottom drawer missing, the other drawers filled with scratchy towels, toiletry items, a couple of white shirts and an extensive collection of buttons.

Opening the last drawer it occurred to me that if Wild

Bill had owned anything of value—a clock radio, a cassette player—the chances were that Mr. Reardon had already confiscated it. I didn't care about those kinds of things, of course. I was only concerned that Reardon, who'd stepped outside to give me a minute alone with my granddad's belongings, had accidentally taken something that might have held a clue to the Wild Bill-Valokus connection.

Oh well. I could hardly question Reardon about that. It would sound as though I was accusing him of stealing.

In the top drawer I found a single yellow pencil and a packet of old yellow index cards fastened by a thick rubber band twisted so tightly it had eaten into the sides of the cards. I undid the band.

That was peculiar. It was a series of lined yellow 5 x 8 index cards. On each one was written a name in some kind of crayon. Mostly black crayon, but sometimes red or purple. They looked like the name cards teachers fasten on young children when they take them as a group to the zoo or museum, to identify them if they are lost.

At first I thought there were names written on all of the fifty cards. But then I realized that only the first five or so contained any writing. No more. The names were:

JOHN SCULLY
LEWIS GIACOMO
BILLY NEVINS
EVAN CONNELL
JACK DUNN

Hmm. A good bet it wasn't a Dixieland band.

That was it. I turned off the light and beat it out of that cellar, knowing that sooner or later there was going to be a rat who could take those half blind cats.

Mr. Reardon was waiting for me outside. He seemed perfectly at ease on that little island, surrounded by the incessant noise of hysterical automobiles. I could see the grime imbedded in his exposed neck.

"You gonna take that stuff away?"

"Look," I said, "I think my grandfather would have liked you to have his stuff. Why don't you take anything you can't use and give it to the thrift shop. It all goes to charity, doesn't it?"

He started to mumble that he didn't believe the thrift shop would pick it up and maybe he was better off just dumping it on the street.

"Whatever you think is best, Mr. Reardon. You've been so nice to help me this way. If I could just ask you one other favor—I don't suppose you could tell me what these are?"

I placed the index cards into his hands. He studied all five of them carefully, miraculously rotating the stump of a cigar from one side of his mouth to the other without using his hands.

"Where'd you find these?" he asked.

"In my grandfather's bureau. Any idea who these people are?"

He flipped through the cards once more.

"Sure I do."

"You do?"

"John Scully lived two houses down. Died last year. And I've known Jack Dunn since we were boys. He used to live on Eleventh Avenue. He's in a home up in the Bronx now. And, hell, Bill Nevins was shot to death more than twenty years ago in his candy store on Fifty-first."

"You mean you can remember the men attached to those names from all those years ago?" I asked.

"'Course I can. Hell's Kitchen was like a small town once upon a time. People knew their neighbors, you grew up and married some girl from the neighborhood, lived on the next block. We felt this place belonged to us. There's nothing left of that now. But in those days that's how it was."

"Any idea why Wild—my grandfather would have those names written down?"

He shook his head vehemently.

"All those men worked on the docks years ago. But your grandad never knew them."

Oh, no? thought I. *I wouldn't count on that.*

The old New York docks had come back into the picture. There was the collection of books at Inge and Sig's place; what appeared to be outdated sailing information in Henry's abandoned apartment; and now this.

"What makes you so sure he didn't know them?"

"Nah. These men were all members of St. Anne's Church, forty years ago, when Father Hogarth was alive. You know St. Anne's Parish?"

"No," I admitted.

"On Forty-fourth Street. It was in a movie once. They used to call it the longshoremen's church. But that was when the docks were a place to work. That was a long time ago."

He handed the cards back to me, shrugging. He had no idea why Wild Bill would make and keep such a list. Unhappily, neither did I.

"Did my grandfather have any close friends?" I asked.

"Just one," Mr. Reardon replied, "if you can call a

rummy a friend. His name is Coop. You'll find him at the Emerald Bar, on Ninth. He cleans up there. And for all anybody knows, he lives there."

The Emerald was a long, narrow place sandwiched between a thrift shop and a bodega. A single small glass window looked out onto Ninth Avenue.

At the bar sat eight old white men drinking Bud from long-necked bottles in synchronized swigs. I watched them for quite a while, waiting for one of them to mess up. But nobody did.

There was a jukebox at the rear of the place. Tony Bennett was singing something, "Stranger in Paradise," my pop had once had the sheet music for. I distinctly remember seeing it in the flip-open piano bench.

At the end of the long bar the room turned left, into an L. There at one of two tables was another old man, reading the *News* in the dim light. He was the only black man in the bar. I assumed this was Coop.

Not one of the drinkers turned around as I walked past. Only the bartender glanced my way, probably deciding whether I looked like a genuinely distressed down and outer who needed to use the ladies room or a junkie looking for a place to fix.

"Mr. Cooper?"

He looked up from the paper but didn't speak.

"Mr. Cooper, I was related to Heywood Tuttle. I wonder if you could spare me a few minutes and answer some questions about him. Someone told me you were his friend."

I pulled out a chair and sat down across from him, even though he had yet to speak a word to me.

"Mr. Cooper, I said—"

"Don't know no Heywood Tuttle."

"Oh. Well, his friends called him Wild Bill."

"Then why didn't you say Wild Bill?"

"Sorry. I'm saying it now. You were a friend of Wild Bill's?"

"Bill's dead."

"I know."

"He dropped dead, on the street. Just fast as that. Stroke, they said. On his way here, I reckon. Said he just fell down dead. Just like that. It just go to show you, when you think you on top of the world, that bastard'll lay in wait for you, throw a big ole brick down from the roof on you. Fore you know it, you dead."

"You mean someone threw a brick at Wild Bill?"

"No, girl, I mean God. I'm just usin' ah example."

"Listen, Mr. Cooper, did you know Wild Bill long?"

In answer, he let go of the newspaper and held up his two hands, at a great distance from one another, presumably to mean the friendship had stretched over many a year.

"Did Wild Bill ever mention a Rhode Island Red?" I asked.

"A red what? . . . Oh, yeah. He mention it."

"Can you tell me what he said?"

Coop leaned back in his chair and closed his eyes.

I repeated my request, but he remained as he was, eyes closed.

At length, it occurred to me what he was doing. Waiting for me to offer to buy him a drink. I got up and went to the bar. The bartender didn't wait for me to order. He placed a bottle of Amstel Light on the bar. Next to it he placed a glass and filled it halfway up with rotgut wine from a gallon jug. I paid for the drinks and brought them back to Coop.

He sipped daintily at the wine but finished the beer in practically a single gulp. Then he smiled and gestured for me to come closer. I moved right next to him.

He put his mouth against my ear and screeched: *"Burrk! burrk! burrk!"*—an earsplitting rendition of barnyard fowl. Then he added, "Girl, you think Bill ain't had nothing better to talk about than chicken."

I controlled my anger and wiped at my ear.

Then I pulled out the index cards and spread them over the table.

"Did he ever talk to you about these men?" I asked.

He drank more wine, surveying the names, shaking his head.

I stood up and started to leave.

"You know," he said slyly, "you look like Bill about as much as old Eleanor Roosevelt do. Least the police and the white man come around here ain't tried to lie and say they related to Wild Bill. Least they don't try to play me for a fool."

I sat down quickly. "I didn't mean to play you for a fool, either," I said. "The police have talked to you—a black cop? Big and mean looking. And a white man who wasn't with the police?"

"That's right."

"When? When did this white man ask you about Bill?"

"About a week before Bill die, maybe less."

"Do you know what his name is? Did he give you his address or his phone number?"

"He give me some of that good brandy is what he give

me. And tell me there's a hundred dollars in it if I can tell him where to find Wild Bill."

"And did you?"

"No. Couple of weeks before Bill die ain't nobody much see him. He was acting mighty peculiar. Might as well have been a shadow for all the time he spent around here. And then, next we hear, he dead."

"What did he look like?"

"You don't know what Bill even look like?"

"Not *him,* not Wild Bill," I said, almost out of patience. "The white man!" I signaled the bartender to fix Coop up again.

So Henry Valokus—and, it sounded like, Leman Sweet— had been looking for Wild Bill a week or less before he died. Valokus and Wild Bill had more than Providence in common. That was for sure. But who really had been hunting who? And which one knew the secret of Rhode Island Red?

I headed north and west, toward St. Anne's Church.

It was easy to find: half the block had been razed. The gray stone church, its steeple rising high and alone, stood sad watch over the street, brooding and yet somehow hopeful. Next to the church was the decrepit building, now all boarded up, that had once been the school.

The youngish, flaxen-haired Finn who turned out to be the current priest at St. Anne's couldn't have been nicer to me. But he could be of very little help.

He took the index cards from my hand and went through them slowly, asking me at one point if I was planning to write a parish history.

"Why do you ask that?" I replied.

"Well, some of these names sound vaguely familiar. But it's probably from the records I've been going over lately. Probably their children went to school here, when we had a school, that is. But this generation is all gone."

The father had no recollection of ever seeing a man who fitted Wild Bill's description either. And no, there had been no gentleman, about so high, with a European accent, inquiring about old parishioners lately.

Everybody in this scenario was mighty interested in ships, in the docks of New York, way back when. That strange roster of longshoremen intersected with a talented jazz trumpeter who ended up a desperate drunk, a mobster who had informed on and then become a laughing stock to his confederates and a crooked undercover policeman. But I had no idea why.

I'd been sitting on the church steps for a good twenty minutes, weary and craving a cigarette, when I noticed the white van across the street. At the wheel was the woman who'd held the gun to my head.

I stood suddenly and beat it back into the doorway of the church. But that prompted no movement from the van. They continued to sit there.

How long, I wondered, had they been following me? All day? And if they were going to try to snatch me again, what were they waiting for? Clearly, if they'd wanted to kill me they could have done so at any time during the last twenty minutes. But they'd chosen to do nothing. Why?

We had a real stand-off going. I wasn't budging from the doorway. And they weren't budging from the curb.

And then, without ceremony, they left. Just drove away.

I spotted the van again near the supermarket. The folks

inside never said a word and never made a move toward me.

I walked into D'Agostino and bought three prime lamb chops, some fresh spinach, and a head of garlic. I went home and put the groceries on the kitchen table. But the moment I opened the bag I realized that I didn't want to eat. I just wanted to sleep. I walked out of the kitchen and collapsed on the divan.

CHAPTER TWELVE

Monk's Dream

Paris.

I am down in the Metro. The Les Halles stop.

I am blowing my heart out. I never in my life ever sounded so grand.

There is not another soul around. Yet my high white silk hat is overflowing with gold coins.

Suddenly the cops show. They are all ferocious Senegalese wearing impenetrable aviator shades. They've come to get me, take me away. And they aren't being gentle about it.

I'm thrown into the back of a van, screaming, protesting my innocence—of whatever the charge may be.

The handcuffs go around my wrists.

You stole those coins! one of the flics shouts to me in his barking-dog French. And he upends my hat and pours all the money into my lap.

I look down at the coins. Embossed on each one is the head of a fierce-looking rooster.

Suddenly all the coins begin to bleed profusely. Within seconds, I have a lap full of warm, sticky blood.

And then the telephone rings!

I had never been so happy to be roused from sleep.

I picked up the ringing phone and heard "Hey, what are you wearing?"

"Ah, come on, Walter. You're making obscene phone calls now?"

He laughed heartily. "No. But I'm planning to be obscene with you in person. Which I hope is gonna be in a few minutes."

"Are you coming up?"

"Not exactly. I want you to come down. You're hungry, aren't you?"

"Of course."

"Okay. There's a hip place on First and First. The steaks are great and this Creole brother behind the bar's got a martini with your name on it. Get on down here. And I want you to wear something nice."

Martini? What was I—a businesswoman? "Walter, are you sober?"

"Not completely. I just feel good."

"Did something happen at work?"

"Just get dressed and get here, Nan. Take a cab. And don't wear no overalls, okay?"

So I grabbed a taxi, driven by, thankfully, a brother who was downright eager to get me in his backseat. He beat out two other cabbies who were heading toward me like ICBMs. We were at First Street—in hippie renewal territory—in no time.

Ooo la la. My lucky night. The French hostess in the leopardskin leotard was glad to see me too. Maybe management would be willing to pay Walter and me a few bucks a night to lend a little dark ambience to the joint.

"Hey, baby." Walter took me in his arms and kissed me, reluctant to let me go, it seemed.

I finally broke from his embrace and took a seat next to him at the bar.

"Walter . . ."

He kissed me again, lightly, on the ear.

I had once accused him of behaving like a jealous housewife, but now it occurred to me that he was doing the classic guilty husband routine—overplaying the love bit because an infidelity was weighing on his conscience. If he pulled a box of chocolates out of his briefcase, I was going to deck him.

The bartender, Creole or not, was seriously cute. I'd take a 'tini from his tapered brown hands any day of the week. He smiled at us and left a little dish of olives next to my glass.

"Mind if we eat at the bar?" Walter asked. "It's private up here."

I looked past his shoulder into the hopping main room. A wave of high-pitched conversation and laughter floated toward us.

"No problem," I said.

"You look good, sweetheart."

"Thank you, Walter. But what's your story? You're a little overstimulated, aren't you?"

He chuckled. "I suppose you're right. I just—I came to some decisions today, that's all."

"What decisions?"

"Number one, I'm quitting the job. Real soon. Another guy at the office—Morantz—Morantz and me, we're starting our own company."

"Well, congratulations . . . I guess. But isn't that going

to be a pretty big deal? I mean, money and offices and staff and all that stuff."

"It's gonna be covered. We've got an appointment tomorrow in Philadelphia. We sign up this client and we got it made. Snatching him right out from under the nose of the firm. And we are going to snatch him. Trust me."

I raised my glass, and my eyebrows, in a wordless toast to him. "And that's why I had to put on a dress?"

"No . . ."

"Walter, you're acting dopey, you know that?"

"Nan, let me ask you something."

"Yeah."

"How many times we split and come back together?"

I looked into his eyes. Maybe I was about to be dumped. But that's not what the eyes were saying.

"Too many to count," I said. "Five—maybe six."

"Gets kind of old, don't it? I mean, we must belong together or something, or we wouldn't keep doing it, right?"

I didn't know how to answer that.

"Why'd I have to put a dress on, Walter?" I asked softly.

"Because I didn't want to ask you to marry me while you were wearing overalls."

Lord!

"Can I have another drink, Walter?"

"So what do you think about it?" he said as he signalled the bartender.

"Shit, man. I don't know. What do you want to get married for?"

Not the world's most gracious response to a proposal, is it? I was sorry the minute the words came out of my mouth. But he went on, undaunted.

"I'm tired of fucking around, Nan. I want us to have a house. I want us to have kids. It's just . . . time."

Kids? *Kids?* I'd never told Walter my thoughts, fears, about having children. I guess, like a lot of other women, or at least I assumed there were many others like me, having children had never been a desire of mine, though I always assumed that if I were to hook up with a man who really wanted them, I'd be able to do my part.

Truth was, I was sure I wouldn't make much of a mom. And I'd always counted myself lucky for having a mother who was so unlike me. I'm self-involved, mercurial, emotionally unstable, don't get any gold stars for patience, something of a loner, apt to take off for ports unknown at a moment's notice, if that, and really don't appreciate people I can't reason with. In short, a child's nightmare. Poor thing would be logging hours on the school counselor's couch before it turned seven, all because of me. But if this theoretical man insisted on babies, at least I could tell him what the deal was going in. Hell, I was better about it than Aubrey. She hated children—with a pure, unalloyed hatred—and would say so to just about anybody.

But I said none of that to Walter. Instead, I took his hand and held it for a long moment.

"Here's what we do," he said eagerly. "I'm renting a car in the morning. Driving to Philly for the meeting. You catch the train at Penn Station and wait for me at Thirtieth Street Station. I'll pick you up at twelve. We drive up to Bucks County. I know this inn you're gonna love. Matter fact, we might spend a few days there once we get married. Anyway, we drive up there, just you and me, have lunch, take it easy, stay the night, just talk about things. Doesn't it sound good?"

Yes, it did. Looked at as nothing more than a little respite from the city, or as a romantic getaway during which we'd plan our wedding (ha, ha), it did sound good.

Wild Bill was dead. Henry Valokus had vanished, probably for good. And the trail of Rhode Island Red was dead cold. I'd been played for a fool, pushed around, threatened, assaulted, fucked and abandoned. And so what was the big issue in my life? Getting married. To quote Fats Waller, "One never knows, do one?"

Walter's proposal had genuinely knocked me on my ass. I had never really known whether I loved him. And I suppose I had never believed he loved me.

So why *did* we keep coming back together? He'd asked a good question.

I tried to visualize myself dusting the living room of some two-bedroomer upstate. Waiting by the garden gate for the little one to come home from school.

Not.

I tried to be a little more realistic: Walt's at work, I'm still in my nightgown at three in the afternoon, listening to Monk records while the pork roast defrosts, maybe noodling a little on the sax or with some spiral bound notebook full of over-ripe verse.

Would Walter want to go to the Loire and sample wines on our vacation? No. We'd wind up in some pricey time share in Jamaica.

"So you gonna marry me or what, girl?" he kissed me again.

I was glad Mom couldn't see me now. She'd have a heart attack from the suspense. I kind of smiled at the image—not the image of her clawing at her chest but the one of her rising off her barstool with the *girl, are you crazy?* look on her face.

"Walter, Walter, Walter," I said, feeling at one and the same time aroused and sad. "I'll tell you what. I'm not going to marry you—tomorrow—but I am going on that honeymoon. And we can talk about it, as you said."

Yeah, "talk" was right. There was an awful lot I hadn't told my little fiancé.

I took the nine-thirty to Philadelphia the next morning. I'd brought four paperbacks along to read on the 90-minute run: a novel by an expatriate American writer with whom I'd spent about ten minutes in bed the last time I saw Paris; a couple of poetry anthologies; and the same unread Gertrude Stein volume I'd been toting on and off trains for most of my life. I didn't crack one of those books. I was much too distracted.

I saw a sign just outside Trenton that seemed to tap on some long buried memory. TRENTON MAKES/THE WORLD TAKES, it read. It made me wonder if perhaps my parents had taken me to Philly when I was a kid. Where could we have been going? Probably someplace exciting, like an interstate spelling bee.

The train stalled just past Trenton and pulled into Thirtieth Street Station at eleven-thirty, a half hour late. Even so, I was still early. Walter had told me to wait for him on one of the benches near the geographical center of the station because he didn't know at what entrance he would find parking for his rented car. I sat down and went a couple of rounds with Gertrude.

At eleven fifty-five Walter had not yet arrived. We were supposed to meet at noon, but Walt is notoriously early.

Meaning that five minutes before the appointed time is late for him. He wasn't there at noon either. And he wasn't there at twelve-thirty.

I tried to remember where he was going in Philly. He was trying to corral a client, he'd said. Clients for Walter were magazine publishers. That's what he did—sell space in magazines to advertisers. But he didn't mention any specific magazine. He just said he and his new partner were going together. What was his partner's name? Mitchell? Mariachi? I didn't remember, and what did it matter? I wouldn't know where to reach them anyway. I couldn't call Walt's New York office—they probably didn't even know he was in Philadelphia. After all Walter and his partner were on a sort of secret mission to help them start their new firm.

I got up and made a circuit around the station. I sat down again. I bought the *Inquirer* and read it. I bought a New York paper and read that. I bought a coffee, keeping watch on the two ends of the station as I sipped it.

It was one-thirty. No Walter. Under my breath I began to curse him in the kinds of terms you don't expect one affianced to use when referring to the other.

I searched out the phones and tried calling Walter's New York apartment. No answer there. And no answer at my own place—just my own voice on the machine.

At one fifty-five I heard the announcement that a train was boarding for New York . . . Last call! It was all I could do to keep my seat. But I managed.

When they made the same announcement forty-five minutes or so later, I succumbed.

I hadn't bought a return ticket. I paid the conductor in cash.

As the train rolled along, my anger dissipated. And in its place came guilt and chagrin and an almighty embarrassment. Why the hell had I gotten so angry at him? Why hadn't I waited? I'd assumed his failure to show up had been volitional, malicious in fact. But any one of a hundred things could have prevented him from being on time. God, he might even have been in an auto accident—or something worse.

Why hadn't I waited longer? Why hadn't I done something else instead of just fleeing? Because I was still Lady Fly Off the Handle; that was part of the answer. I knew another part of the answer, too: I knew I wasn't going to marry Walter Moore.

By the time we got to Newark I had myself a little more in hand. The disaster scenarios were receding from my mind. Surely something had gone awry with Walter's potential client and he was in the station now making frantic calls to me in New York. He'd come back to the city and tell me what happened and I'd make him a nice dinner, or something. And as for the honeymoon, well, one has just got to be philosophical about that kind of thing.

Darn that dream—right, Mom?

CHAPTER THIRTEEN

Friday the 13th

 I was in no mood for the subway. I took a cab home.

The afternoon sun fell dustily into the lobby as I stood fumbling through my overnight bag and all my pockets for my keys. Finally, burrowing at the bottom of my bag, I felt them through a wad of Kleenex. Relieved, I slipped the key into the lobby door and stepped inside.

A meaty black hand covered my mouth so powerfully and so completely that my whole face went numb, my vision blurring.

"Just stay calm, college girl," I heard. "Stay calm and quiet. Somebody's in your apartment and I'm going up to get him. Understand?"

I nodded. The hand dropped away. I turned in the cramped space and found myself staring into the demonic eyes of Detective Leman Sweet.

"Who's in my apartment?" I asked, voice cracking.

"You'll find out soon enough," he said, soundlessly closing the lobby door and drawing his gun. He gestured me backward with the piece. "Stay put."

He was taking the stairs slowly, slowly, the boards creaking faintly as he moved. But before he had even reached the second floor landing, I heard the door to my place swing open. I popped out and looked up after Sweet but I could see nothing but his massive back.

"Police! Hold it!" Sweet bellowed to the intruder.

The words must have escaped the man's throat involuntarily, instinctively: "What the fuck . . ."

"Get your hands up!" Sweet screamed at the man. At Walter.

It had taken me a second or two, but I recognized that voice. That was Walter up there.

What the fuck? My sentiments exactly.

Through Leman Sweet's legs I could see Walt's loafers. I heard a thud and then saw a saxophone case on the worn-out carpet.

"Don't fight him, Walter!" I shouted. "He thinks you're breaking in."

I began running up the stairs, bellowing as I went, "Sweet, leave him alone, Sweet!"

"Shut up!" he yelled down to me. "Stay!" he shouted at Walt. "Don't you move, motherfucker."

The two of them stood in a sweaty frieze, neck muscles taut, eyes locked, until Leman Sweet took a menacing step toward Walt.

"Do what he says, Walter," I warned. But Walter wasn't listening. I don't even think he knew I was there. "For god-sakes!" I shrieked at the detective. "Leave him alone, god-damnit. He's not breaking in. I know him. He's my—"

"I know who he is, girl."

*   *   *

"I ought to kill you where you stand," Leman Sweet growled at Walter. *Stand* was the operative word. He wouldn't allow Walter to sit. As for me, he had said that if I dared move from the kitchen chair, he'd shoot us both.

God help us, I thought at first. It's going to be the Diego scene all over again. Abusive cop beating the hell out of an unarmed citizen. Except my instinct to try to protect poor Walter had suddenly frozen. In one dread-drenched second I had realized that Walt was no innocent bystander here. He was guilty. Guilty of what, I didn't yet know. But it was something a lot more serious than standing up his fiancée in Philly.

"Get that gun the fuck out of my face," Walter came back, blustering, weak.

Sweet only laughed at him. "You got a hot minute to tell me everything," he said. "Don't bother to deny nothing. Don't give me excuses, alibis, nothing. Just tell me what I want to know. Starting with you and Charlie Conlin."

Walter swallowed hard, trying not to come apart, trying to mask the trapped rat quality in his eyes.

Thwack!

Even I felt that backhanded slap across Walt's face. But he took the blow standing up. Then, for the first time since this crazy encounter began, Walter looked at me.

My stomach flipped.

Get a grip, baby girl, said Ernestine. *Here it comes.*

"He had the seat next to me at the Garden," Walter began slowly. "We both had season tickets for the Knicks. We got to talking. I couldn't believe it when Charlie told me he was a cop. He seemed like real people. We liked each other a lot. Started having a drink, shooting the shit after the games. Sometimes I would meet him after work. We used to shoot pool once in a while—pick up—I mean, when I wasn't living with Nanette, he and me met some women at some of the places he liked to go hear music. We were . . . I don't know . . . friends."

"Right," Leman said. "Y'all went out chasing pussy together. Did a little coke together. Shit like that. Real cool. Charlie always thought he was Mister New York Cool. Mister Dangerous. He was going to buy those season tickets even if he couldn't pay the rent. Okay. Go on."

"We had been buddies for a year before he told me about this thing that was going to set us up for life. Charlie had heard these rumors. Unbelievable stories. But he sure as hell believed them. There was this saxophone—they called it Rhode Island Red—and it was worth a million dollars. Maybe even more."

I burst into laughter. Walter must have gone crazy! There was no saxophone on earth worth a million dollars.

"Real funny, ain't it?" Sweet said, not laughing. "You just shut up and keep listening to your friend here. You didn't think it was so funny, did you, Walter?"

"No."

"Keep talking, Walter. Tell us how Charlie filled up your head with dreams of gold."

Gold? What gold?

"He said he had it worked out," Walter went on. "He said people had been looking for this sax for decades, but now he had a line on it. This old man—some jackleg trumpet player—actually knew where he could lay his hands on this treasure. The guy's name was Tuttle but they called him Wild Bill. Wild Bill was tight with Charlie's old lady, a blind girl that he stayed with sometimes. She didn't even know that he was a cop. She only knew him as a musician, Sig, his undercover name.

"Anyway, the two of them, the girl and Wild Bill, would get high together, play on the street together, sometimes she would give him a place to crash, stuff like that. And one day Wild Bill told her about the sax. She never really believed it existed. Tuttle was nothing but an old alkie, used to be a junkie. She figured it was some kind of pipe dream—something he made up.

"She mentioned it to Charlie eventually. She wasn't copping out on Tuttle or anything, she just told him, more like a joke than anything else. Charlie put it all together. He knew then that the rumors weren't crazy, that the million-dollar sax was for real.

"Yeah, he was planning on taking this Wild Bill off—beating him out of this so-called gold mine. But, like Charlie said, what was a guy like Tuttle going to do with something that valuable anyway? He'd never be able to fence it. He was bound to fuck up. Chances are somebody would have either conned him out of it or killed him for it. So Charlie cut himself in.

"He told Wild Bill how it was going to be: he'd give him sixty grand and Wild Bill would turn the sax over to him and be out of the deal forever.

"Wild Bill accepted."

"Yeah," Leman echoed. "I bet he did. But where was Charlie gonna lay his hands on sixty thousand dollars? Simple. He lifted the buy money from the operation we were doing."

"That's right," said Walter.

"Goddamn straight, it is," said Leman. "Then the dominos started falling. Tell us, Walt."

"First, Charlie learned that some washed-up mob punk, an ex con out of Rhode Island, was after the sax. He was a white dude who had been in the joint with Tuttle. Charlie figured, if this guy knew about it, how many others knew?

"Next thing that happened, Charlie got wind that Internal Affairs was about to eat his ass up. They suspected he stole that buy money."

"And that's where I come in," Sweet said, his voice raw. "I didn't know nothing about nothing before IA got in on it. Didn't have to be a genius to realize they were going to fall on me too. I was Charlie's partner, so they figured I was in on it too. If he was dirty then I was dirty. Sure, the nigger in the duo would have to be in on the corruption.

"Finally they were convinced that I was innocent. Next thing I know, the Department's telling me I have to join forces with those idiots in order to find out what the fuck happened to my partner. That's when I started hearing about this stupid saxophone and the bodies it was racking up.

"It must have been touch and go for old Charlie. He was racing the clock near the end. He was hot as hell. A mob guy sniffing around; IA on his tail; dealing with a loose cannon like this old alkie, Tuttle. Isn't that right, Walt?"

"Yes. Wild Bill had told him he'd have the sax in forty-eight hours. Charlie needed a place to stay. He couldn't risk going back to the blind girl's place. And he couldn't stay at my apartment uptown because we didn't want anybody to connect the two of us. He told me to sit tight till he got in touch."

"Right, right," Leman said, a nasty, self-satisfied smile on his lips. "So, of course, that's when you decided to 'involve' your lady friend here."

Walter's eyes flicked over at me and then away. Smart move. Because surely the look I was giving him would have put *his* eyes out.

"That's the way it was, honeychile," Leman said. "Walter sicced Charlie on you."

"I didn't, Nan," Walter said, head down. "I mean, I did, but—"

"Yes, it appears that you did, Walt," I said.

Sweet's grin was ever-widening as he began to speculate. "Charlie picked you up on the street. The two of you were laying up in here having a good old time—"

"Fuck you, Sweet," I said. And I meant it in a way I've never meant that obscenity before in my life. I made a silent vow never to use that phrase again.

He went on, untroubled by my outburst. "—except something totally unexpected happened that night. That night, a little geek named Diego murdered Charlie. And not because of this fantasy saxophone of gold. Oh no. Because of a skinny, blind skank named Inge that he was hung up on. That greaseball kid was probably trying to break in here. Charlie could have heard him and thought it was you at the door, Walter. He opened up, took an ice pick in the throat, staggered back in here and died. Now, ain't that a bitch?"

He paused and wiped his forehead with his free hand.

"Charlie was a pretty good cop," Leman said. "A pretty good crook too. He hid the sixty grand in here before he went to sleep." He looked over at Walter then. "And maybe he hid something else—ain't that right, Walt? Maybe he lied to you and already had the sax. Maybe he stashed that in here too."

"He did no such thing!" I shouted. "How could he have hidden something like that?"

Sweet looked pityingly at me. "Did it ever occur to you while you were running around like black Kojak trying to solve this case that Charlie had put you out that night?"

"Put me out?"

"Drugged you, bitch. The two of you drank a lot, didn't you? The coroner said he had wine in his stomach. Maybe he doped you so he could have all the time he needed to prowl around here. The next day you found the cash in your sax, but not the other sax—not Rhode Island Red.

"So Charlie is dead now, right? What's Mr. Walter's next move, huh?" He caught Walter's eyes but Walter said nothing. "I'll tell you. Mr. Walter figures the money belongs to him now—in fact, everything belongs to him now, whatever he's man enough to find—the sixty thousand, the sax, whatever. So tell us, Walter, what you did about it."

"I don't know what you mean," Walter said quietly.

"Oh really? Wasn't your first step to go to Inge? Makes you kinda nervous to hear her name, doesn't it? Well, we can stop referring to her as Charlie's girl—the blind girl, Walter. Her name was Inge Carlson. Weren't you determined to shake the information you needed out of her? Scare her. Beat it out of her if you had to?"

Walter did that thing again—he swallowed, hard.

Oh no, I thought. No, no, no. Oh no. But I wasn't just thinking it. I was moaning aloud.

"She tried to tell you she didn't know anything about it, didn't she, Walter?" Leman said, sounding almost kind. "No matter what you did to her, she kept swearing she didn't know where the sax was. But you wouldn't believe her."

Walter was shaking his head.

"Is that a 'no,' Walt?" Sweet asked. "You mean no, you wouldn't believe her or no, that's not the way it happened?"

"No," he answered at last, "I didn't believe her. Because while I was searching her place I found a lot of cash. I mean, a lot. I figured she was in on the whole scheme and was cutting me out. She and this Wild Bill were going to cut me out completely. I was nothing to them."

"You were in a real corner, weren't you? You were desperate. You killed her, didn't you, Walt?"

I had been praying not to hear the question almost as hard as I was praying not to hear the the answer.

"I was pushing her around," Walter said, his voice so quiet and thick now that both Leman Sweet and I were straining to hear him. "I was pushing her around and looking all over the place for that sax, or for more money. I had just opened a drawer in the kitchen. I looked up and she had a . . . a pistol in her hand. She could hear me moving around and she had it aimed right at my chest.

"How do you think it made me feel? Beating on a blind girl. I had crossed a line and I knew I was never going back. Just like Charlie had. But was I supposed to let her shoot me to death? I had come too far for that— too far and too close. I picked up that blade and killed her before I even knew it. That dog of hers was going nuts. I couldn't . . ." He broke off into sobs.

"A touching story, bro," Leman said. "Most touching. Did you cry like that when you caught up with Wild Bill and near 'bout killed him too?" He didn't bother to wait for an answer. "He told you Charlie had the sax already, is that it? That Charlie had beaten him to it and didn't even pay him that sixty thousand. You figured then that Charlie had double-crossed you. And then you realized, after all the places you had been looking for it, Charlie had hidden it right here in your girl's place. Meanwhile, Wild Bill obligingly drops dead of natural causes. Looks like you finally got a few breaks, man."

Yes. All Walter needed was a way to get me out of the picture long enough to take the place apart.

"So, asshole, you finally hit paydirt," Sweet said to Walter. "You found it while Miss Bald America here was away from home today. We've been tailing the two of you for a long time now. Watching your comings and goings. If you'd made it out of here before the lady of the house returned, it would look as though she just had a routine robbery. But tell us, what would you have done if she'd walked in on you tearing this place up? Would you have blown her away too?"

I was curious about that too.

"You heard the man, sweetheart," I said to Walter. "Would you?"

He would not look at me. There was grief on his face. Not just shame. Grief.

And even I was ashamed of having asked that question.

Leman Sweet reached around into his back pocket, no doubt going after the cuffs he kept there.

In the half second it took him to do so, Walter made a move.

"Put that fucking gun down," I heard Sweet command. That's when I started screaming.

I'm sure they could hear me screaming on the Champs-Elysées, but Walter didn't seem to.

He turned and ran toward the fire escape, heedless of Leman's shouts.

Walter was at the kitchen window now, where two figures had suddenly sprung up outside. The sight of them was almost enough to halt my screaming. They were the two from the white van, the man and the woman who had kidnapped me, the ones who had held a gun to my head, the ones who had told me about Henry.

Only this time they wore badges around their necks. And their dark weapons, pressed so close to the window, were trained on Walter's forehead and heart.

I saw Walter's arm go up.

"No!" Sweet ordered uselessly, already diving for the floor, taking me down with him.

The windowpane shook and exploded.

All around me the guns spluttered and boomed like amateur fireworks on the beach.

I saw my Limoges café au lait bowl do a freaky dance and finally leap to its end off the corner of the drainboard. And then it was over.

But I was still screaming.

"I hope you're not going to waste no time mourning this motherfucker," Sweet said with a jerk of his head in the direction of the blood-wet body on the floor.

The body. The body. That was no goddamn "body." That was Walter M. Moore. We had made love hundreds of times. Gone swimming in the country. Walked home from the movies. Argued about nothing.

I was sitting at the kitchen table and the detective was perched on the arm of a nearby chair. Someone had placed a glass of water in my hands.

Not stopping to think, not missing a beat, I was on Sweet, teeth bared, crazed. Trying to gouge his eyes with my nails, spitting incoherent curses.

It was the male cop from the white van who pulled me off. Had he flung me or did I slip? I don't know, but I landed on the floor, practically in Walter's arms.

And then, in one movement, I reached for the battered black case that Walt had been carrying. I ripped open the latches and threw back the top so that I could see the million-dollar sax, the thing that so many people had died for.

The three cops rose as one.

I began to laugh wildly.

The case was filled with rusted tin cans.

Leman Sweet looked as if he'd been hit with a baseball bat. He reeled away from the case, looking sick.

The white male cop cursed despondently and sat down across the room.

"Charlie must have filled it up as a decoy and hid the sax somewhere else," the woman cop said.

Brilliant deduction.

Leman didn't have much left after that. The three of them began a half-hearted search of my place, which had already been torn apart. But they seemed to know it was futile.

I wanted to say good-bye to Walter before they called the station and the morgue and the technicians; before the whole surreal mess that had marked the night Sig died started all over again.

I made myself kneel down beside him and touch his brow. Next to him on the thrift shop rug lay his wallet, the one I'd given him for Christmas three years ago.

I could see the tip of his blue plastic Chemical Bank

cash card. For some reason that started the flood of tears again. Walter had always said that if he died suddenly my only responsibility was to empty his bank account and send the money to his nieces in Bayshore.

Was Leman Sweet right? Was Walter Moore, my erstwhile fiancé, a heartless killer? Would he have calmly blown me away if I had walked in on him earlier today?

Maybe. Honey, your taste in men is so bad, anything at all is possible. But what difference does that make now? asked Ernestine, my unbending conscience, my ceaseless voice, my guide, my tormentor, my nemesis.

I saw her point. As far as those two little girls in Bayshore were concerned, what difference did it make?

I slipped the card into the top of my boot.

After they had all cleared out, including Walt, I sat on the kitchen floor and rocked myself like a mother with a wakeful baby.

When I felt strong enough, I called Aubrey, who listened to the whole story without saying a word, and then ordered me to lock up the apartment and get into a cab. She'd be waiting for me at the bar of the Emporium.

It was dark when I left. I didn't hail a taxi right away. First I had to get to a cash machine.

The nearest one was at a funky-junkie corner of Third Avenue. It was not a safe place after dark, but I was beyond fright.

Two derelicts were lying on the floor of the ATM. I stepped over them and inserted the card in the machine.

Walter's PIN number was easy to remember: the numbers translated into "KNICKS."

I punched it in.

The machine asked me how it could help me. I punched the information key to find the balance.

I am working on it, read the display.

Current Balance: $21,415.42.

I stared at the figure for what seemed like hours. I knew that was the blind girl's money in Walter's account. It was like I'd told Henry that day: I got her killed. I gave her that money and I got her killed. Walter. Oh God, Walter. I broke down anew every time I said his name in my head. I was crying not only because he was dead but because he had murdered.

Walter must have been keeping tabs on me, watching me, all the time he and I were apart. Otherwise, how would he have known exactly when Sig was killed?

Internal Affairs had been watching Leman Sweet. Leman Sweet and the other cops had been watching me. Diego watching Inge. Sig watching Wild Bill. On and on it went.

I staggered out, as dazed as any of the lost causes sleeping it off nearby. Everything was crumbling. Sky. Pavement beneath my feet. Little square of plastic in my fist. Looked like it wouldn't be long before there was nothing left of my world.

I needed sanctuary, even if that meant a screaming neon palace of flesh. I needed to get to Aubrey.

CHAPTER FOURTEEN

'Round Midnight

Where the hell was I? All I knew was, I was wearing a fur.

Oh, right. The Emporium. Aubrey had put me to bed on the fold-out cot in the dressing room.

The clock near the small sink read three o'clock. In the morning or the afternoon?

In a few minutes Aubrey came in, naked from the waist up and wearing a spangled G-string: that casually perfect, taut, amber body glistening. She took a clean towel from the back of a chair and began daintily to blot away the sweat.

"You awake, Nan?"

"I'm awake. How long have I been sleeping?"

"About five hours. I gave you a pill and you went out like a light."

"Walter is dead, Aubrey. They shot him."

"I know, baby. You told me."

"He was doing some terrible things . . . terrible things, Aubrey. I didn't know."

I lay the coat aside then, and noticed that I was wearing

a clean, starched shirt. I stared down at the whiteness of it, not able to remember changing my clothes.

"Here, Nan, take this." Aubrey had opened a cabinet next to her dressing table. She handed me a glass and half filled it with brandy. She lit a cigarette for me as I drank.

We sat without speaking for a while.

"He asked me to marry him, Aubrey. I didn't even get a chance to tell you."

"Well," she sighed, "that's Walter. You know one way or another he was gonna leave your ass at the altar."

I laughed once, bitterly. Then I broke down. She let me sob, periodically feeding me Newports and Courvoisier.

And at last the tears stopped. I felt oddly clear headed, light. I got up and washed my face carefully.

"Is that bartender who used to deal still here?" I asked. "The one who used to get you the Demerol?"

"You mean Larry? Yeah. He's on till four. Why you asking?"

"Does he still buy and sell things?"

"What things?"

"Pills. Stuff. Just about anything you can name."

"Yeah, I guess so. But I asked you why you wanna know."

"Because. Like Walter said, I've come to a few decisions. Could you ask him to come in here for a minute? Tell him I need to talk to him."

"Don't do nothing stupid, Nan."

"Please get him."

"Don't do nothing stupid," Aubrey repeated when she walked in again with the brown-eyed bartender. "Larry, you remember my friend Nanette, don't you?"

He nodded.

"Hey, Larry, I need a gun," I said.

"No shit?"

"No shit. Can you get it for me?"

He looked over at Aubrey, who rolled her eyes and walked into the toilet.

"Can you get it?"

"What do you mean—tonight?"

"Why not?"

"What do you need?"

"I just said, Larry, a gun."

"I mean *what kind*, angel."

"It makes no fucking difference whatever."

He scratched his head, looking me up and down.

"Larry, let me be honest with you. You're dealing with a novice here. I just need a shooting device that works. Something that will make an impression, something that will threaten and persuade. Something capable of killing a rat, for instance."

"There's a nice .22 long I can lay my hands on right away. Comes with a full clip."

"What's a .22 long?"

"Well, it certainly could take out any rat who tried to fuck with you."

"Can you show me what to do with it?"

"Sure."

"Is there a cash machine near?"

"On Chambers Street."

"I'll meet you out front at four."

The white shirt felt good against my skin. I wriggled into a pair of Aubrey's snakeskin leotards, stretching them over the mass that is my butt. I put my boots back on and, at her insistence, threw on Aubrey's fur coat. I got a glance at myself in the mirror. My God, I could have been looking at Tookie Smith! Or I might have been a downtown money bunny off for a long day's shoe buying and gallery hopping.

"Why don't you wait for Jeremy?" Aubrey offered just as I was leaving. "Come home with us. He gonna be here in a minute."

I shook my head. "Tell him about Walter, would you? Just tell him—just say hello from me."

I withdrew five hundred dollars and gave Larry four hundred of it.

Larry lived in a nice loft building on Nineteenth. He came out of the kitchen carrying a mid-sized Dean and DeLuca shopping bag. He placed the bag on the floor and removed my gun.

A gun is a singular thing, isn't it? Nothing else in the world even remotely resembles it.

"Long" was right. I was surprised at the size and heft of it. I got a five-minute lesson on how to operate my new purchase. Clip. Safety. Barrel. Muzzle. Ammo. Push this up. Pull that back. "This looks like the foreskin on a very angry penis," I remarked.

"Uh . . . right," said Larry.

"Thanks for everything, Larry. I never met you before in my life."

He nodded. "Looks like you dropped a few pounds since the last time I saw you, didn't you?"

"I guess."

"Looks good on you."

"I've got to be running along now, Larry."

"Well, just a second."

"What?"

"You're really not going to do anything stupid, are you?"

"Do I look stupid?"

"Not at all. Listen— How about staying for a drink?"

"It's almost light," I said. "I have to go."

I pushed through the prison grey lobby doors and stepped out onto the deserted street.

It had begun to rain.

CHAPTER FIFTEEN

Reflections

I made myself a lovely breakfast: poached eggs, sliced oranges and wafer-thin toast without the crusts. Next to my plate lay my big black gun, just north of my coffee cup.

I'd been in the house alone for a couple of days. Aubrey and Jeremy had been wonderfully supportive and loving but I hadn't wanted to see them. Or anybody.

I felt better today though. It was almost noon. I had slept well. The apartment no longer terrified me. It simply was no longer such a big deal that both Sig and Walter had been slaughtered in close proximity to this cute little vintage enamel table, a genuine piece of 1930s Americana, that I'd always loved decorating with my West African dolls and beeswax candles and ecru damask placemats.

Besides, something told me that once the management office got wind of the goings-on of the last few weeks, I wasn't going to have the opportunity to grow old here, savoring the memories of the good times had by all in this place. The super hadn't even *looked* at me while he replaced the window, wordless, lips tight.

I did the dishes and cleaned up the last of the mess from the shoot-out and subsequent ravaging of my home.

Question for the day: Where was Henry Valokus? Not near his old place, was my guess. In other words, nowhere close to where I lived and did my street music number. No, the chances would be too great that he and I would meet in the neighborhood.

He had been nosing around a seedy bar at Ninth Avenue and Forty-fourth Street—hardly the street of dreams, more like rue de Wino—looking for Wild Bill. Looking for that golden sax. Rhode Island Red. It sounded like enough money to take the sting out of tramping around Hell's Kitchen. Henry might have dedicated his days, and even his nights, to combing the neighborhood in search of Wild Bill, might have hung out in bars no self-respecting Hell's Angel would have taken a leak in. But I knew Henry would not live in Hell's Kitchen. Even if they were auctioning off Bird's jockstrap in the Italian bakery on Fifty-first Street.

Actually, the thought of Henry picking his way up and down the ragged steps of a Tenth Avenue tenement was almost funny. Goodness, where would he have his caffe latte in the morning? Where would he find that Russian leather soap he was so fond of? Where would he get his yellow roses?

So where was Henry living? Assuming he was living.

He had said once that as much as he liked the Village, he thought it was too precious. The Upper West Side drove him crazy, he said; everyone was either eighteen or eighty or insane, and the streets were always clogged with people. He got a kick out of prowling Fifty-second Street because it had been the site of so much astonishing, wonderful music, the old Birdland having grown in his imagination to high temple status. But every trace of that era had vanished. At present, the neighborhood was nothing but black glass corporate high-rises and overpriced eateries and luxe hotels.

Where was he right now? Where was he living while he went on searching for Rhode Island Red? And how much time did I have to find him before he either located the saxophone or gave up and left town?

I got out my New York City map, unfolded it on the table and suspended my hands, palms down, above its surface, as if it were a Ouija board, as if it might suck my finger down to the exact spot where he lived. Of course, he might be in Chinatown, or Morningside Heights, or Queens or Jersey City. But I was banking on his having remained in central Manhattan.

"Henry, you are right . . . *here.*" I zoomed in on a section of the map, grabbed a pencil and circled the area.

There wasn't a lot of mystery involved in my selection. I knew he had to be somewhere between Thirty-fourth Street and Seventy-second Street—where he was comfortable, in the heart of the city—shops, food, music, wine, gifts to impress a lady—all within easy reach—transient hotels galore, anonymity.

I put on some Erik Satie, for a change of pace from the Billie songs to commit suicide by, a change from the junksick Parker ballads and the postdesolation Bill Evans stuff. It's funny how heartbreaking Satie can be, and at the same time soothing, focusing. And then he'll go off on one of those surrealist tangents, where he sounds like a spoiled brat having a tantrum, or the inside of a mad trolley conductor's head. He was one weird-looking man, Satie. I think I probably would have had a lot of fun with him.

I moved into the living room and smoked one of Aubrey's horrendous Newports with my second pot of coffee. From where I sat I could see the lethal-looking barrel of the gun on the kitchen table. *An angry penis?* Poor Larry. Had I really said that to him? I'd have spat on a weakass, cornball line like that just a few weeks ago.

I had to hurry up and flush Valokus out into the open before it drove me completely crazy.

What would bring him out? What would force him to surface?

Not a great new Indian restaurant. And, alas, not me.

The fabled million-dollar sax? Definitely. But that I couldn't deliver.

All morning I'd had an idea brewing for a little fire sale that Henry would not be able to resist. It wasn't Bird's jockstrap or his pickled brain or the last Camel from the pack he bought on the morning of his death.

No, none of those things.

I closed my eyes.

How did Henry, who had an awful lot of free time on his hands, spend his day? Lingering over coffee. Bathing. Lunch. Shopping for new CDs and old records and . . . stuff. He went on meandering walks. He went to green markets looking for the freshest fruits. Flower shops. The butcher with the tenderest veal. In fact, one of my many favorite things about Henry was how much time he'd been willing to devote to my comfort: He was constantly in the supermarket shopping for the delicious dinners he was going to make me. I guess to the average man Henry must have appeared pretty faggy. But God, did I appreciate his ways.

And now I had to hook into those mundane aspects of

his life, kind of pretend to be him. I thought maybe I had a
way.

The phone rang, breaking my concentration. I let it go
for a long time, trying to decide whether or not to answer.
Finally, I picked it up.

It was my mother, checking on my mood. She wanted to
show sympathy but didn't want me brooding too much
over Walter's death.

Mom didn't know anything like the truth about Walter's
death. The cops had managed to keep it out of the papers.
And in the version I'd given her, Walter had been an unfortunate bystander in an attempted liquor store hold-up.

After five minutes or so of consolation, she moved on to
lighter topics. Guess who she'd run into at the Grand
Union, for instance.

I couldn't possibly.

Paula Stratton's mother, of all people.

I gave up, finally, and she had to tell me who Paula
Stratton was.

"*Paula*," she insisted. "Your old friend from high
school."

"Oh, right," I said. "Paula."

Who hardly qualified as an "old friend." It was only that
Paula, who was white—as most of the kids were at the
high school I attended—had been an unfortunate fat girl,
not the same kind of outsider as I but with some little
sparks of admirable weirdness over and above the
poundage. Our bonding during freshman and sophomore
years had been more defensive than instinctual. We went to
plays and concerts and movies together, spent a semester
abroad together, because no men were interested in taking
us out. By the time Paula and I were seniors, however, she

had a marvelous little figure and had lost interest in just about every arcane pursuit the two of us had ever shared.

"Do you want her number?"

"Whose number?"

"Paula's number," Mom repeated patiently. "Her mother says Paula had a pretty bad time of it with that husband of hers, but now she's single again and going to law school and—"

"What's the number?" I made believe I was writing it down.

I interrupted her again a few minutes later. "Mom, I'm going to be away for a while."

"Away where, Nanette?"

"I think I'll go visit a friend in—on Cape Cod. I need to get away from here. I'll call you when I get back."

So that was the one millionth and first lie I'd told her in my life.

I went in to the kitchen and refilled my coffee cup, glancing once more at the ugly weapon on the table and returned to the other room.

I put pencil to paper.

This, I thought, will be my landmark poem.

The first line was a snap.

LEAVING NEW YORK! MUST SACRIFICE.

The second line was even easier.

FOR SALE!

And in a minute the rest of it just fell into place:

HIGH-END STEREO EQUIPMENT: LIKE-NEW AIWA COMPONENTS
SOLID MAPLE CABINETS

And then the wow finish:

ALSO FOR SALE—78S, LPS. ECLECTIC. RARE STUDIO AND
BOOTLEG HOROWITZ, PRICE, LENYA, DIZZY, BIRD, MILES.

And the coda:

CALL 000–0000. LEAVE NAME AND PARTICULARS. SPECIFY
YOUR INTEREST. WILL SEND POSTCARD WITH PRICES,
DETAILS.

I sat back and stared at my handiwork.

Was I or wasn't I the Rimbaud of the fire sale?

Now, what phone number could I use? Not mine. Val-okus would recognize it. Not Aubrey's. Not anyone's who knew me.

No. It would have to be an old-fashioned answering service. That was easy. I looked in the Yellow Pages and found one, taking care to see they didn't even have the same exchange as my own number. I called them and was quoted a modest fee for the service. That's all I needed. I said I'd drop by and pay them in person in a few hours.

Then I took another piece of paper and rewrote the message in larger, bolder lettering.

What next? What next? Xerox it. How many would I need? How many laundromats and supermarkets were there between Thirty-fourth and Seventy-second Street— between Second and Ninth Avenue—that have accessible community bulletin boards? Hard to know. A hundred and fifty copies would be safe.

I rushed downstairs and made the copies. The moment I entered my apartment again, the phone started ringing.

This time I didn't answer. It rang eleven times and was silent. It could have been my mother again. It could have been Aubrey or the cops. It could have been danger. I pulled the plug out of the wall.

I had more work to do: placing ads that read exactly the same as my notice in every giveaway neighborhood newspaper I could think of and in the *Village Voice*.

I wouldn't be going to Cape Cod. But I had decided it would be best to get away from my apartment for the duration of the gig.

I got together my toothbrush and some assorted cassettes, my Walkman, my sax and packed my Afghani carpetbag. I wrapped the gun and ammunition carefully and added them to the bag.

Sixty minutes later I was lying on a queen-size bed in a lovely room in the Gramercy Park Hotel. My windows looked out on the stately, deserted park with its high iron fences.

I had for years, one season flowing into the next, walked past the pristine hedges of that park, its empty benches calling to me. But Gramercy Park was private. You couldn't enjoy it unless you were one of the lucky and well-heeled residents of the immaculately kept townhouses ringing the park. The elitism of it had always bitten my butt, but now, for as long as I lived in the hotel, I was one of the haves, one of those fortunate few entitled to sit or stroll there any time I wanted. All I had to do was ask the hotel doorman to unlock the gate.

Maybe, I thought, I will play my sax there, treat the neighbors to a free concert. It made me laugh. Somebody would lean out of their french windows and see a big, short-haired Negress mangling Ellington favorites on a beaten-up sax. I'd see how fast the police responded to that one. I decided to forget about the park for the present.

By three in the afternoon I was on the road, so to speak. Nervous about leaving the weapon back in my room, I was toting it. Strapped, as they say. I wondered briefly, giddily, madly, whether today would be the day I would happen upon a crime in progress, let alone be the victim of one. I was just demented enough to play avenging angel. You talkin' to me?

My route was simple. Walk to Ninth Avenue. Then go north on Ninth following it uptown when it turned into Amsterdam, around Lincoln Center, up to Seventy-second Street, posting my notices as I went. Then turn around, cross the street, and go south on Ninth to Fortieth.

My aim was to place a "For Sale" notice in each laundromat and supermarket and friendly-looking small shop that would accept it. After Ninth, I would walk up Eighth Avenue, then Broadway, then Seventh Avenue—and every other avenue east to Second. I figured it would take the rest of the afternoon and early evening and the next couple of days. Of course, a great swath of streets in midtown had virtually no markets or residential service stores of any kind.

On the way to my kick-off point I used Walt's bank card to get another five hundred dollars; I purchased a large box of pushpins and two scotch tape dispensers, and paid the telephone service.

It was wearying work. About two out of every three laundromats had an open bulletin board, and about one of every three supermarkets. Many of the notice boards were chock full of babysitting, catsitting, and word processing offers. I had to rearrange subtly and then tack or tape, or both.

In a small supermarket on Madison and Sixty-eighth Street I ran into a slight problem.

There was a non-busy bulletin board just inside the entrance. No one was by the board so I started to tack up the notice, just as I had in dozens of other spots.

"Just hold on a minute!"

I turned. A tall, hunched white man, a real Silas Marner type, was standing about two feet away. He was wearing a shirt and tie and one of those old-fashioned blue grocer's smocks. His breast tag read: Manager.

"What are you doing?" he whinnied at me.

"I'm placing a notice on the bulletin board," I said as if speaking to a two-year-old. "See? This is a sheet of paper and there's writing and everything on it."

"You can't just come in here off the street and do something like that. I've never even seen you in the store before. Do you shop here?"

Fat chance.

I didn't answer.

"I don't suppose you live in our neighborhood?"

I didn't answer.

"You're probably working some kind of confidence game. Here! Let me see what you've written."

He grabbed the notice out of my hand and began to read it.

Without saying another word, I opened my purse and shoved my hand in. My fingers went slinking around the grip of the .22.

Then I released the weapon and pulled my hand out fast. I really was slipping over the line. There was a pretty serious law against what I was about to do. I was flirting with a mandatory one-year jail term just for carrying this fucking thing. A concealed weapon. What was I doing? Jeopardizing everything to teach a racist creep a lesson.

I turned on my heel and walked out. Mister Manager was still holding my notice. He could do with it as he pleased.

Two mornings later I concluded my rounds. By way of

celebration, I went into one of those fancy bookstores with an espresso bar attached and bought a new biography of Proust, a coffee table–type volume about the great jazz vocalists, a guide to North America's wild flowers, and what was being touted in the papers lately as a new wave murder mystery. I took them all back to my room and hit the bed reading.

There was a not bad jazz club a few blocks away, on Third Avenue, where I'd gone for a drink my second night in the hotel. After I napped, bathed and changed, I headed over there.

I wore a gray knit dress, tight and clinging. Nazi bitch high heels. Two black guys and three white hit on me. I was spending money like water. After all, whose money was it? The little girls in Bayshore? It was nobody's, really. Walter had stolen it from Inge. Inge had gotten it from me as a gift. I had received it from Sig. Sig had stolen it from the NYPD, who'd gotten it from criminals, or from the taxpayers, perhaps. Hey, maybe it was my money after all.

For the next couple of days I read and waited and went to movies and bars, either the club on Third or the funky place down on Houston, or the lounge in the hotel, where a Johnny Hartman wannabe warbled throughout the night. I contacted no one. I did not return to my apartment.

On the third day after that I showed up at the offices of my telephone service. I was handed eighteen messages, responses to my notice and ads.

Three asked for descriptions and prices for everything.

Eight asked me to send descriptions and prices for the stereo equipment only.

Four wanted the records alone.

Two asked only about the Horowitz recordings.

And one caller wanted only the Charlie Parker stuff.

My hands shook as I held the pink message slip. It could have been anyone, this caller. Any one of a million Parker buffs. But oh, I knew it was Valokus. I knew it.

How did I know? The caller gave his name as Rodney Dameron. An obvious phony that combined the name of the white trumpeter in Bird's quintet—Red Rodney—with the name of the elegant pianist Bird had worked with in his early days—Tadd Dameron.

Maybe Henry was every bit as dumb as Justin Thom had claimed.

Mr. "Dameron's" address was on West Fifty-seventh Street. Judging from the numbers, it was between Eighth and Ninth avenues. He gave his apartment number as 810.

I got into a taxi.

The Daisy Chain Inn was part of a nationwide franchise of motels that seemed to run the gamut from family getaway to nightmare crack house, depending on whether the inn was located in Orlando or Watts. This one was medium grimy. Maybe a little hooking going on, but nothing too heavy.

I sat there in the cab, across the street from the dirty blue canopy, for fifteen minutes or so, thinking that, maybe, a miracle would occur and I'd see Henry going in or out.

That didn't happen, of course.

I told the driver to take me to the Gramercy Park Hotel.

Once in my room, I dialed Information and got the number of the Daisy Chain Inn. I called. I told the operator I wished to speak with one of his guests: Rodney Dameron. "He's in room 810, I think."

"Just let me check," I was told. He put me on hold for a

few seconds and then came back on the line. "Yes, that's right. I'll ring him."

"No, don't bother," I said quickly. "There's my other line. I'll call back."

I took my gun out of my bag and rubbed it along the quilt in a kind of burnishing stroke. I'd gone over Larry's instructions a hundred times, wondering if I'd ever understand the lure of these cold and weighty enigmas called guns.

Mine was unloaded now; the clip was in the bureau drawer. But I'd logged a number of hours over the past few days standing in front of the vanity mirror and studying myself as I slid the weapon in slow motion from my purse; as I aimed it and pouted like Faye Dunaway in *Bonnie and Clyde*; as I held it at my hip and pretended to be Wyatt Earp; as I ran from one end of the room to the other spraying imaginary bullets and grotesquely mouthing the word "muthafuckaaah" like a drug dealer in one of those death-in-the-ghetto movies.

I lay down on the bed, the Proust book open on my stomach. Damn, what I wouldn't give for a warm madeleine just about now. And a cup of china black from that piss-elegant tea shop on the rue Christine.

My mind drifted back to the afternoon Henry and I had spent making love, drinking a shamelessly overpriced bottle of wine from the Loire and looking at a book of photographs of Paris in the 1950s. What if we'd met then? I'd asked him, being whimsical. Perhaps, I'd speculated, he'd be a soldier of fortune and I an emigré beatnik. We'd spend our days drinking bitter coffee and collaborating on books, and our nights listening to Juliette Greco in the darkest café in town.

This is why I love you, Henry had said when my flight of fantasy was exhausted. Your imagination. I wish you could have met my grandmother.

Before I knew it, I was asleep.

I swallowed my ethics and went into the park that night. I sat quietly on a bench, switched on my Walkman and listened to a tape I'd patched together months ago—Bud playing "Parisian Thoroughfare," Lady's exquisitely rethought "These Foolish Things," Coltrane's version of "Violets for Your Fur;" you know, the old goodies. I allowed myself to get thoroughly chilled, so that coming inside again would be all the sweeter.

I had a beautiful, if lonely, dinner: a little liver-onion-tomato turnover and a tandoori chicken to die for, and to all intents and purposes the entire bottle of the creamiest white Châteauneuf de Pape I'd ever pulled from a vintner's shelf.

I walked back slowly to the hotel and went directly to the elevator bank, across from the piano bar. I pressed the up button.

Just as the elevator doors opened, a song flew out of the darkened lounge and stabbed me in the back of the neck.

Lord, why do good pianists use "Funny Valentine" like a weapon, like Cupid's arrow dipped in grief?

I thought at that moment—well, I was thinking many things at that moment. Please God, make it all not true. Make Walter alive again. Let me be at home drinking coffee from that big yellow cup I love. Please God, let me turn around this minute and see Henry standing there, healthy, grinning, explaining, arms out to hold me against the heady, oaken scent of his soft blue overcoat. Please God, if you can't let me forget him or forgive him, then let it feel good when I blow his damn kneecaps off tomorrow. Please God, if I don't find somebody to talk to—be with—tonight, I'm going to pass away from loneliness.

Help me, Ernestine. Tell me what to do.

"You like jazz, Mr. Thom?" I asked.

"Take it or leave it," he said. "Who is this?"

"I met you a few days ago. You know, the smash-up in love with the asshole from Rhode Island."

"Aubrey's friend! What's happening, Nanny?"

But before I could tell him, he went on: "I'm usually better than that with voices, being an old bartender. But my trick was to put a face with the voice. You don't sound black on the phone. No offense, but, know what I mean?"

"Yeah. Hoover said the same thing when I called to warn him about the Panthers."

"What do you need tonight?" he asked after an appreciative chuckle. "The answers to tomorrow's mafia quiz?"

I didn't speak for a minute.

"Hello?" Thom called into the receiver.

"Yeah, I'm here, I'm here."

"Where's 'here,' Nanny?"

"A bar. At the Gramercy Park Hotel."

"You didn't find asshole there, did you?"

Again, I fell silent.

"Hey, smash-up, you still there?"

"Yes. No, asshole's not here. I'm calling for you—to thank you for your time. How about a drink?"

"At that old folks home?"

"Sure. There's a little brown boy singer goes on soon.

His feet haven't touched the ground in fifteen years and he's real cute."

"I didn't think you knew any of my people, girlfriend."

"Oh, Mr. Thom, *you're* the one from Indiana, remember? Not I."

I had time to fix my make-up and walk around the block a couple of times before Justin's cab pulled up at the door of the hotel.

I reached into the taxi window and paid the fare before he had a chance to.

"Nobody has paid *me* to do anything in a long time," he said as we went through the revolving door of the lobby. "You made my fucking night."

"No problem. I'm flush."

"Sold your story to the *Enquirer*?"

"No. I've turned to crime—like everybody else. The bar's this way."

We settled in with our drinks—Dewars with a water back for Justin, Grand Marnier for me.

I had called Justin Thom out of some weird survival instinct. Somehow I knew it was him I needed to talk with tonight, not Aubrey. Justin, though he baited and patronized me, had become a confidant. But with a twist: There was only so much I could tell him. I had to hold certain things back, in a word, lie. The miraculous things was, he knew that, and yet here he was.

"How bad a bad guy are you, Justin?" I asked after a few minutes of small talk.

"What do you mean, sweetums? Sex or the job?"

"The job. You know, you work with some pretty persuasive people. You kind of have to do what they tell you, right? I mean, what I'm asking is have you ever—"

"Killed? Me? Oh, child, please! I run a tits and ass joint and make sure the bartenders don't steal them blind. It's just a job and a pretty good one, considering. Come to think of it, it's too bad your boyfriend couldn't just look at it that way. You'd both be a lot happier now if he had."

"Henry, you mean. Yeah, maybe so. But I don't see how our paths ever would have crossed if he had just been one of the boys."

"You'd be surprised, baby. A lot of them that look like cute Mr. Guido from Jersey have got them some brown sugar on the side. And would kill anybody who messed with it."

"Well, that's nice for them. But I don't want to be nobody's 'on the side.' "

Justin snorted. "That's something only a smash-up would say. I'm an aging homosexual. Wasn't for the side, I'd never have a boyfriend."

I toasted him with my snifter, deferring to his wisdom, but not swallowing it whole.

We fell silent when the good-looking singer made his appearance. "Girl, he *is* special," Justin whispered to me. "I knew Aubrey wouldn't have any dumb smash-ups for friends."

After the set was over, I asked the bartender to freshen our drinks. I felt there was so much more to say to my new buddy, but I didn't know how to say it. So I sat listening to his horror stories about life in the closet that is Indiana, and the glory of stepping off the Greyhound and into the seamy Times Square night lo those many years ago. I guess Justin needed a buddy, too.

"What did you really want to tell me tonight, Nanny?" he said at last.

I shook my head. "I don't know. Maybe I wanted to run my lecture on Charlie Parker past you."

"That would be a waste."

"Why? Who do you like?"

"Luther."

"Figures," I said, laughing a little. "Henry likes jazz a lot, you know. That's kind of how we met. If I ever see him again, there are a couple of . . . old records I want to give him."

"I bet. I bet that's why you're trying to hunt him down."

My hand was creeping involuntarily toward my purse. It was all I could do not to take out the gun and show it to Justin. But I wasn't sure what the point of that would be. Did I want to show him how tough I was or did I want to beg him to take it away from me and bury it somewhere? Was I asking him to endorse my plan or talk me out of it?

I withdrew my hand and turned the bag clasp side down on the bar.

"All I can say is, he's lucky it's you and not Aubrey," Justin said, laughing diabolically.

He reached over and handed me one of the paper napkins from the pile next to the container of maraschino cherries. My eyes were a little wet. I hadn't even known it.

We sat through another show. The singer blew a kiss our way at the end of his last number. Justin caught it and put it in his breast pocket.

It was late.

"Well, thanks for the date, Nanny," he said as I called for the check.

I removed a hundred-dollar bill from my bag and pushed it toward the bartender.

Justin took note of it and smiled. "Scared of you."

"You should be. Not too many unemployed smash-ups throw around bucks like this," I began, "but I only—"

"Never mind," he interrupted. "You know what the president say—'Don't ask. Don't tell.' "

"Good night, Justin. Kiss Aubrey for me."

It was very late. And I had promised myself I'd get to bed early. Tomorrow was going to take just about all the strength I had left.

But on the other hand, what difference did it make? I knew I wouldn't sleep.

CHAPTER SIXTEEN
These Foolish Things

 I went to the flower market, to a small stall just around the corner from the apartment where Walter murdered Inge. I bought two dozen yellow roses at the wholesale price. Our lady of the flowers, all in black. That was me. I had on the same Norma Kamali that I'd worn to my grandmother's funeral, and the much prized leather jacket Aubrey had bought me when one of her mysterious investments went platinum. The little felt cloche hat I had bought just two days ago. If I looked like a mob widow who also happened to be a fashion model, so much the better. On my wrists were the cheap leather bracelets that had belonged to Charlie Conlin.

On the cab ride north, up Eighth Avenue, I tried to settle on an opening line. What, exactly, would be my first words when Henry opened the door? Would I have the gun already drawn? It was a tough call. Besides, I couldn't stop thinking about Walter this morning. His touch. His breath. His laugh. Those goddamn WASPy loafers of his, with all that blood on them, floated across my vision again and again.

All the death. All the devastation. The violence. The be-trayals. I was of it now. Walter had made me part of it. Henry had made me part of it.

If I could have it all back the way it was before this in-sanity started, here's what would happen: I'd sit Walter down over a hamburger and a beer and tell him it wasn't going to work out for us, the best thing he could do for himself was find himself another woman. And as for Henry, our affair would begin at a smoky club somewhere. I'd go out with him for a while, sleep with him, travel with him, live with him, love him with my life.

But that was all make believe. The reality was that Wal-ter was dead. The reality was that Henry had tricked me, used me, wrecked my life—shit, I was ready to blow a hole in his neck because of all those things, wasn't I? And yet the reality was that I still loved him, and maybe I wanted to blow the hole in him because of that too.

My history with Walter, my passion for Henry, my guilt and rage—all of it jumbled and boiled and bubbled over there in the back seat of that taxi.

I stood on the curb outside the hotel until I could pull myself together, then I went in.

The sleepy, balding man behind the desk rubbed at his eyes as he watched me approach, as if he thought this lady in black with all the yellow flowers might be part of his dream.

"Mr. Dameron ordered flowers?" he asked after I'd stated my business.

The concierge looked a little confused and I didn't blame him. It was only a quarter to seven in the morning.

"No," I said with a Mona Lisa twist of the mouth. "They're from me."

He regarded me for a moment and then, finally getting it, tentatively returned the smile.

"I'll just call up." He reached for the phone at the edge of the counter.

"No, don't," I said softly, placing my hand over his. "It's a surprise."

Concern clouded his face for an instant. And I took the opportunity presented by that second's worth of hesitation to place a folded twenty in front of him.

"It's 810, right?"

"Yes ma'am. 810."

I took the elevator up.

The Inn was still sleeping. I could almost hear the collective toss and turn of every sleeper behind every closed door, breathing gagged and heavy, dreams troubled, saturated with last night's mistakes.

I leaned on the bell of 810 and kept up the pressure until I heard shuffling from within.

"Yes? Who's there?" he called, sounding crazy in that roused from sleep way.

I mumbled an utterly incomprehensible response that ended with "the front desk."

He repeated, "Who's there?"

And I repeated the same nonsense syllables, but much louder this time, and with an edge of high-handed impatience.

He bought it. There was the sound of the safety chain sliding away from its cradle, and then the click of the dead bolt.

The door swung open a second later. And before he could speak again, I thrust the flowers into his arms.

He was wearing dopey patterned flannel pajamas, looking for all the world like a kid who'd misplaced his teddy bear.

"Very hot look, Henry," I said, stepping into the room and slamming the door closed with my foot.

"Oh. It is you, Nanette. How beautiful you are."

I swung the palm of my hand, which by now held the gun, against the side of his face. It connected just right.

Henry reeled backwards and staggered until his legs gave way beneath him and he was sitting on the factory outlet carpet. The long-stemmed yellow beauties were still in his arms. He had not raised a hand against me nor tried to fend off the blow.

I pointed the gun at his stomach. He blinked once, then looked away.

I waited. And waited.

"Nothing to say, Henry?" I spoke at last.

"Yes, my love. I do have something."

"Good. What is it?"

"I would like to have a cigarette."

"Oh sure, baby. Sure. Here, let me light it for you."

I walked over and kicked him in the groin.

The roses went flying. He lay flat on his back, gasping for air, beginning to cry.

"Uh uh, Henry. None of that. Sit up straight like a good boy."

"Why have you come here, Nanette? Surely there is nothing you could want from me now."

"It's story time, Henry. I want a story from you. Tell me about Rhode Island Red."

"It will not help you to know. It will only—"

"Henry, do you believe that I'm prepared to pull the trigger on this fucking thing and walk out of here without a backward glance?"

"I do not know."

In answer, I pushed the safety catch to the off position.

"What about now?" I asked, holding the weapon straight out in front of me.

He sighed. "All right. But I truly do wish to have a cigarette. May I?" He nodded toward the coffee table where the packet of Dunhills lay.

"Go ahead."

After he'd taken his first draw, he raised one hand gingerly to the wet slash at his temple. The blood pulsing out of it was like a miniature stream carrying debris.

"Before I tell you your story," he said, "I want to tell you something else."

"I don't want to hear anything else, you bastard."

"But I will tell you anyway," he pronounced calmly. "I know how angry you are. But how many times can you kill me?"

He had me there. I fell silent.

"It is true that I used you in an inexcusable way. It is true I have no right to even hope for your forgiveness—in this world or any other. But it is also true that I fell in love with you . . . Yes!" he shouted as I began to smirk. "No matter what you do to me and no matter how terribly I betrayed you, I won't have you say I didn't love you."

"Okay. Fine. That's out of the way. Now tell me about Rhode Island Red."

"In a moment. I will in a moment."

With some effort, he rose off the floor then, my weapon trained on him, and regathered the flowers into a bouquet. "Will you allow me to put these in water?"

"For godsakes, man!"

But he was already at the small tin sink.

The roses gave off a brilliantly sad light in their empty stewed tomatoes tin.

Henry called over his shoulder, the tap still running, "How old are you, Nanette? I never thought to ask."

"What are you—kidding?"

"No, my love. I want to know."

"Don't call me that again," I threatened.

He shrugged.

"I'm twenty-eight. How old are you—were you?"

"And so I am already dead for you?"

"What do you think, Henry?"

"Yes, I know. Well, at least you see why it doesn't matter so much to me that you may kill me. I suppose that is the way it was always meant to be—that someone would kill me. What difference does it make who does it? Coffee, my—I mean, Nanette?"

I could see that he'd filled a cheap tin espresso pot with water and was scooping out coffee grounds from a brightly colored can.

I strode over to him, plucked the can from the kitchen counter, and threw it against the nearest wall.

That did me in. That was my last little explosion of bile.

I sat down heavily in one of the ugly tufted barrel chairs and shook my head. "Listen, Henry, do you have an Uzi hidden in the milk or something? I mean, are you going to catch me off guard and blow me away before I can get you?"

"Don't be insane! I love you!"

"Whatever. Because if you are, I guess I don't really give too much of a fuck either. Just make the coffee and get back over here and talk. And do something about your motherfucking head! You're bleeding all over the stove."

Henry had changed into a dark brown turtleneck and black trousers. On the fake wood coffee table, the ice cubes inside the hotel wash cloth he had used to staunch the blood dripping from his wound melted one by one.

I sat smoking one of the Dunhills, not speaking, watching his lips move, refusing to cry, wanting his mouth on me, hating myself.

"You know almost as much as I do now," he said. "But you don't know the history. The story, as you say.

"As you can see, I do not have the thing called Rhode Island Red. I will never have it. I know that now. I don't know where it is. I just know that it's gone. Gone—again.

"It is so much like you to think you could go to the library and find out what you need to know about criminals. You cannot, Nanette. Any more than I could expect to absorb this—what?—this essence of a great black musician by listening to his music and worshipping his image."

Henry looked depleted, sick around the edges. His eyes were swollen from the two-way crying jag we'd had in the bathroom.

"And when you could find nothing from the books, to think that you walked into the lair of this lieutenant . . . Tom . . ."

"Justin Thom," I corrected, no life whatsoever in my voice. "And he's hardly a lieutenant."

Suddenly he was rushing over to my chair, eyes wet again. He tried to take my hand, kiss it.

"Don't!" I pulled my fingers out of his grasp, shaking my head violently. "Just don't."

Slowly, he backed away from me and onto his own seat again.

He continued. "In your research did you read of a man called Tonio Abbracante?"

"I don't know. Perhaps."

"He was a hard man. A mafioso. As bad as they come. Long ago, it was he who controlled everything in Providence. In the late 1940s and early 1950s.

"He may have been a vicious criminal, but first he was a man. And one day he fell in love with a woman. A different kind of passion than he had known before. For a different kind of woman. She was a rich and beautiful lady from Newport who had fancy horses and fancy ancestors.

"Abbracante was not content to have an affair with her. He wanted to marry her. To this woman he probably represented excitement, adventure. Or perhaps the only reason she ever gave him the time of day was to scandalize her family. To rebel. Who knows what she really thought of Tonio? He may have been nothing but a clown in her eyes.

"One thing about this lady, though: she was absolutely fearless. Fearless enough to play with Tonio Abbracante as if he was no more than a college boy suitor. Tonio never stopped asking her to marry him. And finally she relented. It was a very foolhardy thing to do. In a way she set her own doom in motion with that acceptance. She said she would marry him if he could get the great Charlie Parker to play at their wedding.

"Can you imagine it? She'd marry him *if* he persuaded Bird to play at the wedding! As if he were on the same level as the caterer or the seamstress who sewed her veil.

"She may have been mad, but she was interesting, this woman. She made Tonio understand that Parker would have to come—or be enticed to come—of his own free will. That Tonio must not threaten him in any way. For if he did, not only was the wedding off but their relationship would end. Period. He must *persuade* Bird. She must have known it was an impossible task.

"Abbracante was an ignoramus about music. He likely had never heard of Parker and could not have cared less about his genius. But he wanted that woman. He did what had to be done.

"From his ranks he chose a trusted underling to be sent as an emissary to Parker. It could only help that this underling loved music and had been an amateur guitarist.

"That man was my father.

"Needless to say, Bird laughed in his face—the first time. But Abbracante was persistent. He would buy Bird or die in the effort. After all, he was a criminal, and he knew that every man has his price. After trying just about everything else, he sent my father to a pawn shop to buy an ordinary saxophone. Then he filled the saxophone with pure heroin and soldered the top shut, and all the stops, with gold. He offered it to Parker as the fee for one night's work.

"Parker accepted. It was the one lure he couldn't walk away from. And so he played at the sumptuous wedding.

"For a little while Tonio Abbracante was happy in the unlikely marriage he had made with the woman who had so obsessed him. He had gotten what he wanted.

"And about eighteen months later he had her murdered. No one seems to know why.

"Shortly after that, my father must have offended Tonio. Because he killed him too.

"Parker was set to tour Europe a few days after the wedding. He was to go over by ship. At the last minute, the tour was canceled without explanation. Bird had been spotted at the dock. But no one could explain why, at the last minute, he refused to sail. The theory is that he canceled because the sax was stolen from him somewhere on or near the ship.

"There were a dozen whispered stories about what happened that day. Rumors. Nothing was ever proved. But the most likely one said the theft had been engineered by a group of New York longshoremen.

"I was no more than a boy then, of course. After my father was killed, I was sent back to Greece to live with my widowed grandmother. My poor mother must have believed that that was the only way to keep me out of the life of crime that had killed my father. She was wrong. By the time I was twenty-five I was back in the States and eager for all the things I thought the mob could provide me with. Money. Women. A beautiful car.

"But it was a disaster, start to finish. Not only was I the world's worst criminal, no one seemed to understand that I had been raised in Europe and would naturally be different, strange to them. They made fun of my manners, of the way I spoke English, of my interest in music, and so many other things. I was called a homosexual, a fool, a coward.

"Of course I spent a fair amount of time in prison. Where else could my life have led me?

"And then, during one of my many terms, I met Wild Bill. He was a difficult man, but a decent man then. And I grew to like him. If nothing else, we had music in common.

"It turned out we did have more than that in common, though. We spent many hours talking about the legend of this golden saxophone called Rhode Island Red. And he told me he knew the waterfront in Manhattan like the back of his hand. That he had contacts in Hell's Kitchen. And that he had a lead on some of the longshoremen suspected in the theft. When he got out he was going to New York to find it. And we would be partners.

"I'm sure you don't know what prison life is like. Most of the time you'll talk about anything, do anything, simply to relieve the boredom. The chances were a million to one that Wild Bill was ever going to get the sax. Most likely he was living in a dream world and had no clue how to find Rhode Island Red. But I believed him, because I needed to.

"And against all the odds the miracle happened. He actually located the horn. But he forgot about me. In the end he couldn't hang on to what he'd found. Someone took it from him. And now everyone with even a remote connection to the horn has been destroyed. My one and only consolation is that I did not kill anyone for it.

"It shouldn't be hard to write the ending to this story yourself, Nanette. When I found out about the man you were involved with, I had to discover how much you knew about the sax. I couldn't know how I would come to feel about you.

"What I should have known is that I'd never have Rhode Island Red—or probably much of anything else. I'm a gangster without a gang, I've run out of money, I have no friends, no work, and . . . well, I . . ."

"You no longer have me. Is that what you were going to say?"

He merely nodded, out of words now.

We sat in silence while the city came to life eight stories

below. The autumn sun grew steadily stronger, like a patient taking surer and hungrier sips of broth.

About eleven o'clock. Henry fell asleep.

There was one question he hadn't answered. But I knew why: He didn't have the answer. Where was Rhode Island Red now? Had a corrupt Internal Affairs cop snatched it? Was it in a flophouse in Hell's Kitchen? At the bottom of the Hudson, still leaking poison after forty some years? Still killing people and their dreams.

Wherever it was, I hated it. Hated it for the way it had poisoned all our lives. For the sleeping greed it had wakened in good people like Walter and Sig. For the freaky way it had destroyed my chance for happiness with the man who sat across from me snoring softly, while I held his life in my hands. He trusted me. Jesus, it was all so stupid.

I found myself wondering whether Bird was in heaven or hell. And was he laughing now, or crying.

I stood and retrieved my coat and bag. I took the gun out, examined it one last time and headed over to Henry's chair.

I rested the barrel on his shoulder, perhaps an inch from his ear.

He slept on for a while, but then he must have sensed me there. His eyes fluttered open.

"This is for you," I told him. "I think it's time you learned a trade—my love."

The hotel lobby was no busier than when I'd arrived nearly five hours ago.

The clerk I'd bribed gave me what I guessed was his sexy look and hailed me winningly. "Well, hi there. Was he surprised?"

"No," I said, regretfully. "He wasn't a bit surprised."

More
Charlotte Carter!

Please turn this page
for a
bonus excerpt from

COQ AU VIN

available in Hardcover from Mysterious Press
in February 1999

CHAPTER 1

Travelin' Light

 Damn, I was tired. My saxophone seemed to weigh more than I did.

I had awakened early that morning and immediately commenced to fill the day with activity—some of it necessary, but most of it far from pressing.

I played for a time midtown, a little north of the theater district; made some nice money. That wasn't my usual stomping ground. I had picked the corner almost at random. I don't know why I did so well. Maybe the people had spring fever, hormones working, calling out for love songs. In fact the first song I played was "Spring Fever." When you play on the street, you never know why you're a hit or a bust. Is it the mood of the crowd? Is it you? Is it the time of day or the time of year? Anyway, you do the gig and put your money in your belt and move on.

Next, I power-walked up to Riverside Park and played there for a while; did my two hours' volunteer

1

work at the soup kitchen on Amsterdam; bought coffee beans at Zabar's; took the IRT downtown; bought a new reed for the sax on Bleecker Street; picked up some paint samples at the hardware store; then played again on Lower Park Avenue, closer to my own neighborhood.

Makes me sound like a real flamer, doesn't it? A go-getter, a busy bee. Not true. I'm lazy as hell.

What I was doing was trying to outrun my thoughts. That's what all that busy work was about.

Over dinner the previous night, the b.f. (the shithead's name is Griffin) had announced, number one, he wouldn't be spending the night at my place because he had other plans, and number two, he had other plans . . . period.

I should have known something was up when he said to meet him at the little Belgian cafe I like in the Village—the other side of town from my place. He hated the food there, but it was convenient for his subway ride home.

This kind of thing has happened to me before. The relationship is at some critical point—or maybe not—maybe it's simply that a certain amount of time has passed and I'm re-evaluating it. I meet his family. Mom wants to know if this is "the real thing." I'm asking myself constantly, Is the sex really that good? Should I stay in or should I get out?

And then, a couple of weeks later, before I come to a final decision, he splits.

What's with that?

I always seem to end up asking myself that question. What is with that?

I didn't spend the night crying or anything. I merely came in and stripped out of my clothes and snapped on the radio and finished whatever brown liquor I had in the cabinet. Temper tantrum aside, breaking the porcelain planter in the living room window had been more of an accident than anything else.

Sleep was a long time coming. Yes, I had decided about 2 A.M., the sex *had* been *that* good. And when I awoke in the morning, I just started moving like this—manic.

Now I was exhausted. I packed up my sax and started the short walk to my apartment near Gramercy Park.

Our homeless guy was back. It had been so long since anybody had seen him on the block, we all figured he was dead. But here he was again, in a neck brace, evil as ever, begging for dollars and cussing at anybody with the nerve to give him coins. "Why don't you comb your hair?" he called after me when I stuffed a single into his cup.

I made a quick run to the supermarket and then into the benighted little corner liquor store where a white wine from Chile is the high-end stuff.

I had poured myself a glass, turned on the radio, and read through the mail before I remembered to check the answering machine.

"Nanette, it's me. About tonight. You're still coming over to eat, aren't you? Because I've got something to

3

tell you. It's— I'm—Well, I'll tell you when you get here. I'm going out now to pick us up some food at Penzler's. You still eat pork, don't you, baby?"

Mom!

Oh shit.

I had forgotten. Two weeks ago I had said maybe we'd have dinner—I walked over to the kitchen calendar—tonight.

I was in no mood to see anybody tonight, let alone Mom, for whom I'd have to put on an act—make out that things were fine between me and Griffin, and that my fabulous—and utterly fictitious—part-time job teaching French at NYU was going great. I'd have to be careful never to mention the sax or my street friends or anything remotely connected to my career as an itinerant musician on the streets of Manhattan. She might have been able to handle it if she ever found out that the teaching job was a lie (I was getting steady translation work, at least). But she would have gone absolutely crazy if she knew I blew sax on the street corners with an old fedora turned up to catch the cash. *And* I'd have to haul my ass on the F train out to Queens.

Well, I just wasn't going to make it. Not with all these papers to grade. Not with this pneumonia, cough cough. Not tonight. Tomorrow maybe, but not tonight.

I've got something to tell you.

I turned that gossipy, girlish phrase over in my mind. What was there about that locution that troubled me so? It didn't sound like Mrs. Hayes, that's

4

what. It just did not sound right. And, come to think of it, there was a bit of a quaver in her voice too.

Oh, God. She's sick. Heart. Cancer.

I rushed to the wall phone and dialed her number. No answer.

I threw my jacket on and locked up.

Halfway to the subway, I realized I was probably being crazy. There were only about three million other reasons my mother might have had to sound worried. Maybe it really was something about her health, but that didn't have to mean that death was knocking on the door.

So why hadn't she answered the phone? She was probably still at Penzler's, Elmhurst's answer to Dean and DeLuca, inspecting the barbecued chickens and braised pork chops and waiting on line for a pound of potato salad. Or out in the back yard. Or over at the Bedlows' house, picking up one of Harriet's cobblers for our dessert.

By then I was at Sixth Avenue. I turned downtown instead of north to the Twenty-third Street station. It was a spur of the moment thing. I had suddenly decided I needed a drink before heading out there, and I needed a little reassuring from the one person whose level head and unfailing equilibrium I could always depend on: my one and only homegirl, Aubrey Davis. Who works as a topless dancer.

We knew early on, at about age nine, that I was the whiz at sight-reading music, inventing lies more believable than the truth, and forging my mother's signature. "Very bright, but a bit unfocused," one of my teachers had told Daddy on parents' night.

Aubrey, however, was the one to call when you wanted to see some dancing. She struggled mightily to teach me one or two moves. But it was no good. I could work the shoulders, and I could usually work the hips too—just not at the same time. To this day, when I hit the dance floor I look like a hold-up man who realizes too late that his victim is carrying a taser. By the time we were fourteen we'd both thrown in the towel on my dancing career.

It was about that time, on a summer day, that Aubrey's mother abandoned her. She went off to play cards with some people and just never came back. In school, I was the brightest star in the heavens, but Aubrey, when she deigned to join us, was the butt of the kids' pitiless taunting—about her clothes, about her poverty, about her mother, and in time, about her morals. The oddsmakers wouldn't have laid ten cents on Aubrey's chances of getting through life in one piece. They'd have lost. She is a genius at taking care of herself. And my girl never wastes a second looking backward.

Anyway, Aubrey is now one of the bigger draws at Caesar's Go Go Emporium, which is exactly the kind of place it sounds like, tied however circuitously to the mob and located in that one dirty corner of Tribeca where Robert De Niro has not yet bankrolled any emigré restauranteurs.

She performs topless, like I said, and what she wears over the nasty bits is barely worthy of the term *panties.* Between weekly pay and tips she makes a pretty impressive salary, only a fraction of which gets declared to the tax folks. I don't know all the details, but I believe Aubrey has an enviable little portfolio going, thanks to one of her Wall Street admirers. I could always hit her up for money, but I made a vow long ago never to do so unless I was literally starving. See, if you ask her for a couple of hundred, the next thing you know, she's putting down a deposit on a new co-op for you. She is that generous. She is also a great beauty, and I love her madly. So does my mother, who took turns with the other grownups in the neighborhood in trying to raise her.

I heard the pounding bass line from halfway up the block. Caesar's. I hate that fucking place. I hate the white men in their middle management ties who come in for their fix of watery scotch and flaccid titties. I hate the rainbow coalition of construction worker types in their Knicks T-shirts drinking Coors and spending their paychecks on blow jobs. And I've got zero patience with all of them. Not Aubrey, though. She understands men—all kinds of men. And boy, do they love her and her Kraft-caramel thighs and her cascades of straightened hair and her voice like warm apple butter.

It is little wonder that Aubrey became a superstar, if you will, at Caesar's. A lot of the other dancers are distracted college girls who'd rather shake their ass in a dive than work behind a cosmetics counter somewhere, or they're skanks strung out on crack and pills. But Aubrey, who isn't even much of a drinker, is focused, engaged, thoroughly there when she's dancing. She has a fierce kind of dedication to her work, and the guys seem to pick up on that immediately. It is the damndest thing, but they appear to respect her.

There was no one on stage when I walked into the darkened room. The girls were taking a break. I walked double time through the crowd of horny men, and had almost made it back to the dressing rooms when I heard a male voice call my name. My whole body stiffened for a few seconds. I kept walking, but the voice rang out again: "Hey, Nan!"

I stopped and turned then. I couldn't believe that any man who actually knew me would not only be hanging in a place like this but would actually want me to *see* him in here.

To my relief, it was only Justin, the club manager. He was standing at the end of the bar, his signature drink, dark rum and tonic, in one hand and one of those preposterously long thin cigarettes in the other. Justin, self-described as "white trash out of Elko, Indiana," is Aubrey's most ardent fan. Of course, his admiration for her has no sexual dimension; he is as funny as the day is long.

Justin has a benign contempt for me that actually manifests itself as a kind of affection. I'm just not a femme—his word for a certain kind of lady that he idolizes. (Femmes, you see, are a subgenre of women in general, all of whom he refers to as "smash-ups.") In any case, he is absolutely right—I am no femme: I don't sleep all day, as Aubrey does, and then emerge after sundown like a vampire. I never paint my nails, I don't own a garter belt or wear spike heels before nine P.M., my hair is Joan of Arc short, I don't consider the cadging of drinks one of the lively arts. I don't share his and Aubrey's worship of Luther Vandross, and, probably my worst sin, I cannot shake my body. The truth is, he thinks I'm overeducated and a secret dyke. Justin does not understand going to college and does *not* approve of lesbians. But he likes me in spite of himself and, giving the devil his due, he says my breasts are "amazing." We've been out drinking together a couple of times, once just the two of us and once with an old lover of mine, an Irishman who is still turning heads at age forty-two. Yeah, Tom Farrell garnered me quite a few Brownie points with Justin. On the other hand, Griffin, my ex, met Justin once, and the two of them scared each other half to death.

I saluted Justin, raising a phantom glass to his health, and continued walking backstage.

Aubrey gave out with one of those Patti Labelle-register shrieks when she saw me swing through the door. She was busy applying some kind of sparkly shit all over that flawless body and she didn't have one stitch on.

"Christ, Aubrey. Put some clothes on," I said. She made me feel like I had the body of a Sumo wrestler and the skin of Godzilla.

"This just makes my night! What are you doing here, sweetheart?" She slipped into a peach-colored robe as she spoke.

"I just thought I'd drop in for a minute on my way

9

out to see Moms. Is there anything to drink back here?"

"Yeah, just a minute." She walked to the door and called out into the ether: "Larry, get me a Jack Daniel's, baby. Tell him don't put no ice in it."

The glass was in my hand almost before I could blink. I took a healthy drink from it.

"You look kind of funny, Nan," she said. "Wait a minute . . . don't tell me that nigger is trifling with you again?"

"No, it's not Griff. It's my mother."

"How is Moms?" she asked me, back at her dressing table.

It was taking me a long time to answer. "What's the matter with her, Nan?"

"Probably nothing," I finally said.

"What does that mean?"

"I know you're going to say I'm crazy, but . . ." I repeated, a bit abashed, the phone message that had set me spinning.

"Nanette, you *are* crazy, girl. How you know it ain't something good instead of something terrible? She could be getting married again for all you know."

"Aubrey, I know you're a relentless optimist. But give me a break, huh. Moms is getting married? To who?"

"How do I know that?"

"Or me, for that matter."

"That's what I'm saying, Nan. You don't know all her business."

I took another deep drink of the bourbon. "Trust me, it's not wedding news."

"Okay, fool. She's not getting married. But that still don't mean she got cancer, do it?"

"No, you're right, it doesn't. But I'm still a little freaked. Which brings me to the reason—another reason—I came here. I thought if you could get a couple of hours off tonight, maybe you'd go out there with me."

"Oh shit. I can't, baby. I *am* taking some time off tonight—but I gotta meet somebody for a couple of hours."

"Oh." It flitted through my mind to ask who she was meeting, but then I remembered myself, and who I was talking to, and who she worked for. I didn't want to know any of the particulars. Of course, it might have been something perfectly innocent, but I thought I'd better let it go.

I stayed a few minutes longer, until it was almost time for her to go on again. She insisted on having one of the guys run me out to Queens in his car. I ran through my head the possibility of staring at the thick neck of some club gofer while I sat in the back seat all the way across town and then over the Long Island Expressway to Elmhurst. Or maybe, I thought with a shudder, he might try to chat me up. We'd talk about—what?—Heavy D's latest, or some new designer drug? My heart sank.

Then I mentally put myself on the subway, stop after stop after stop. I didn't even have a newspaper to distract me.

I went for the car.

I left with the promise that I would call her the next day to give her a full report on Mom's news, whatever it turned out to be.

On the way out I ran into Justin.

"What's happening, Smash-up?"

"Same old, Justin. You know."

"Have a quick one with me, girlfriend."

"I can't."

"Got a date?"

"Yep. Dinner. With my mother."

"Ooooh. Bring me back some cornbread."

I guffawed. He didn't know how funny that was.

The kitchen was spotless, as always. But then, why shouldn't it be? Mom never cooked. Everything was take-out or premixed or delivered in stay-warm aluminum foil.

"Mom, I'm here! Where are you?"

My mother's cotton dress was as surreal as the kitchen counters in its neatness. Decorous page boy wig bobby-pinned in place. Makeup specially blended by one of the black salesladies at the Macy's in the mall.

It must be eight, nine years now since Daddy left her. But if I no longer remembered the exact date that had happened, Mom sure did. I bet she could tell you what she'd eaten for breakfast that day, what shoes Daddy was wearing when he broke the news to her. On those rare occasions when Mom talks about him, she never uses his name, referring to my father only as "him."

My father soon remarried: a young white teacher on his staff at the private school where he was now the principal. Outside of the occasional birthday lunch, Christmas time, and so on, I saw very little of him. He was happy enough, I suppose, in his new life. And he never missed an alimony payment.

"Nanette, what have you got on your feet?"

"They're called boots, Mother."

"Those things are something you wear down in the basement when you're looking to kill a rat. Don't tell me you dress like that for—"

"Holy mackerel, Mother, what is it you have to tell me!"

"It's about Vivian," she said grimly.

I fell into a chair, suddenly exhausted. No melanoma. Thank God. No wedding.

Vivian, my father's sister, had been my idol when I was a kid. Breezing into town and swooping me up, Aunt Vivian meant trips into Manhattan and eating exotic food and hanging with her hip friends and my first sip of beer and every other cool thing you can imagine when you're ten years old and your father's baby sister is a sophisticated sometime-fashion-model who drinks at piano bars and parties with people who actually make the rock 'n' roll records you hear on the radio.

My father felt about his little sister Vivian the way Justin feels about dykes. He disapproved of her friends and her nomadic ways and her prodigious consumption of vodka and her way-out hairdo's and everything else about her lifestyle, which he didn't understand at all.

My mother didn't understand it any better than he did, but she loved Vivian just the same. Maybe that was due to the same kind of sympathy with strays that had moved her to take Aubrey to her heart. Mom looked on with pity while Auntie Viv blew all her money and drank too much and got her heart broken by trifling pretty men and then recovered to start the cycle all over again.

In time Vivian married and divorced—two or three times, if I remember right—and moved out of New York and then back again, half a dozen times—to L.A. and Mexico and France and Portugal—wherever the job or the party or the boyfriend might take her. Daddy and she had one final royal blowup during the cocaine-laced eighties and stopped speaking to each other altogether. We didn't even know where she had been living for the past eight or ten years.

And now, apparently, some disaster had befallen her.

"Is she dead?" I asked. "How did it happen?"

"No, no. She isn't dead."

"She isn't? Then what happened to her? What about Vivian?"

"She's in trouble. Wait here a minute."

Mom vanished into the dining room.

I sat looking around the kitchen in puzzlement, at last fixing on the covered styrofoam plates that held our dinner, waiting to be popped into the microwave.

And I thought the day had been long and weird *before* I crossed the bridge into Queens. What the hell was going on here? Well, at least my mother hadn't tried to reach me at NYU. That sure would have resulted in an interesting phone message. But I had always discouraged her from calling me at work, telling her that as a part-timer I didn't really have an office of my own.

"Look at these."

She handed me two pieces, one a standard tourist postcard with a corny photo of the Eiffel Tower, the other a telegram.

I turned the postcard over and read:

"Long time no see. Hate to ask you but I'm strapped. Can you spare anything? Just send what you can—if you can. Love, Viv."

The postmark on the card was about three weeks old.

There was an address beneath her signature. A place on the rue Cardinal-Lemoine—my Lord, Viv was in Paris.

I looked up at Mom and began to ask a question, but she ordered me to read the telegram first, which was dated a week or so after the postcard.

"JEAN: DID YOU GET MY CARD? WORSE. I CAN'T GET OUT. VIV."

"What's this about?" I asked, the fear rising in my voice.

"I don't know, honey. I don't know." Her spine stiffened then and her eyes took on a glassy look. "I finally called . . . *him*. I mean, he is her brother."

15

"You're kidding! You called Daddy?"

She nodded.

I tried to imagine White Mrs. Daddy picking up the phone in their apartment near Lincoln Center. Handing the receiver over. Jesus, the look on his face when she told him who it was.

"What did he say?" I asked. "Did Viv write to him too?"

"Yes. But he doesn't want to know anything about Vivian. Says he tore the card up without reading it. It's a sin. I told him I hoped one day he would be hurting in the same way and when he reached out for help—well, never mind. I told him I think it's a sin, that's all."

I shook my head. "Wow. This is so weird. What are you going to do? You don't have any money to send her, and if Pop won't do it—"

"He wouldn't give it to her, but I managed to shame him into giving me something for you."

"Me? What do you mean?"

She pulled out a chair for herself then and sat down in it before answering. "Listen, Nan."

"What?"

"I don't have any money to spare. But—well, I do have it, but it's not mine. As a matter of fact it's Vivian's money."

"What are you talking about, Mother?"

"I mean I actually do have some money for Vivian—especially for her. When your grandfather died he left most of what he had to your daddy, naturally. And you got enough to take that beautiful trip. But

16

you know how he was. He feuded with Viv just like your father did, but at the end he wanted to come to some kind of peace with her. Nobody even knew where Vivian was at the time. So he left her some money, and gave it to me to keep for her. It's in a special account. Waiting. There must be close to ten thousand in it by now."

"Ten thousand dollars! That sure sounds like enough to bail her out of trouble. And you mean you've had this money all along?"

"Yes. I knew sooner or later we'd hear from her again."

"But not like this," I said.

"No. Not like this. And so . . ." She glanced away from me then.

"What is it?"

"I know it's a lot to ask, Nan. You haven't seen Viv since you were a kid. I just know she's over there drinking, broke, stranded somewhere. Maybe even sick. I wouldn't know where to begin to help her. I don't know how I'd even get out of the airport over there. But I thought—since you've been there so many times—I thought maybe you could go over there and help her—take this money to her and help her get home. Like I said, I managed to shame your father into giving me enough for your expenses."

Expenses?

"What are you saying, Mother? You want me to go to Paris!"

"Yes. Would you do it? If— I mean, only if you

could take the time from work. You're going to be on spring vacation soon, aren't you?"

"It started yesterday, Mom. No problem."

A lot to ask! *Holy*—

I felt a kick right then. Right on the shin. I knew who that was: my conscience, Ernestine. I just kicked the bitch right back. Yes, I'm a liar, I told her; a deceiver, a cold-hearted Air France slut. I was thinking not of my Aunt Viv in a French drunk tank but of the braised rabbit in that bistro on the rue Monsieur le Prince.

A lot to ask? Coq au vin, here I come!